Cover Art Courtesy of Edee O'Meara

Turtle, 1994
Acrylic on paper
14" x 23"

Gatherings V

"Celebrating the Circle"

Recognizing Women and Children
in Restoring the Balance

GATHERINGS:
The En'owkin Journal of First North American Peoples
Volume V - 1994

Published annually by the Theytus Books Ltd. and the En'owkin Centre for the En'owkin International School of Writing

Canadian Cataloguing in Publication Data

Gatherings

Annual

ISSN 1180-0666   ISBN 0-919441-61-0

1. Canadian literature (English)--Indian authors--Periodcals.
2. Canadian literature (English)--20th century--Periodicals.
3. American literature--Indian authors--Periodicals.
4. American literature--20th century--Periodicals.
I. En'owkin International School of Writing.
II. En'owkin Centre.

PS8235   C810.8'0897   CS90-31483-7

Managing Editors:	Beth Cuthand and William George
Associate Editors:	Gerry William, Kathleen Wootton, Jeannette Armstrong, Greg Young-Ing
Page Composition:	Marlena Dolan, Anna Kruger, Chick Gabriel, Linda Armstrong
Proofreading:	Anna Kruger, Chick Gabriel, Gerry William, Linda Armstrong and Ann Snyder
Biographies:	William George
Cover Design:	Marlena Dolan
Cover Art:	Edee O'Meara

Please send submissions and letters to 'Gatherings', c/o En'owkin Centre, 257 Brunswick Street, Penticton, B.C. V2A 5P9 Canada. All submissions must be accompanied by self-addressed stamped envelope (SASE). Manuscripts without SASEs may not be returned. We will not consider previously published manuscripts or visual art.

Copyright remains with the artist and/or author. No portion of this journal may be reproduced in any form whatsoever without written permission from the author and/or artist.

Typeset by Theytus Books Ltd. Printed and bound in Canada

Copyright 1994 for the authors

The publisher acknowledges the support of the Canada Council, Department of Communications and the Cultural Services Branch of the Province of British Columbia in the publication of this book.

Table of Contents

Introduction:
Two Voices Beth Cuthand and William George   1

WATER

Christopher David
It Has Rained For A Million Years - Poem   6
Odilia Galvan Rodriquez
Star Nations - Poem   7
A. Rodney Bobiwash
Creation - Poem   9
A.A. Hedge Coke
Resonance In Motion - Poem   11
Raven Hail
Mage Is Magic - Poem   16
Raven Hail
The Ruby Necklace Story   17
Roma Potiki
Snake Woman Came to Visit - Poem   20
Roma Potiki
to tangi - Poem   22
Trixie Te Arama Menzies
Karanga - Poem   23
Jack D. Forbes
Mama God - Poem   24
Kateri Damm
True Rock Woman - Poem   26
Jane Inyallie
Moon Rite - Poem   27
Jean Wasegijig
Searching - Poem   28
Valerie Dudoward
Rising Sun Woman - Poem   29
Valerie Dudoward
My Rain Is Rain - Poem   31
Louise Halfe
Not Defeated - Poem   32
Louise Halfe
For Blankets and Trinkets - Poem   33
Beth Cuthand
This Red Moon - Poem   34
Victoria Lena Manyarrows
The Moon Is Our Messenger - Poem   37
Colleen Seymour
Were You There - Poem   39

Kimberly Blaeser
Those Things That Come To You At Night - Poem   43
Jose Garzia
Stars, Tadpoles and Water - Poem   45
Don Birchfield
Contributions of Choctaw Woman to Choctaw History - Essay   47

EARTH

Victoria Lena Manyarrows
America/Love Song to the Native Lands - Poem   54
Peter Blue Cloud
Autumn Morning - Poem   56
Gerry William
The Ogopogo - Story   57
Odilia Galvan Rodriguez
Widow's Clothes - Poem   64
Jan Bordeau Waboose
Survival - Poem   65
Henry Michel
Paved Memory - Story   66
Arlene Marie Beaumont
Home - Poem   71
George Anderson
Grandma - Memoire   74
Janice Acoose
In Memory of My Koochum Madeline - Poem   77
Darril Guy LeCamp
The Midnight Caller - Poem   79
Sheila Dick
Crosswords - Poem   80
Leona Hammerton
Long Ago and Now - Poem   81
Armand Garnet Ruffo
The Green Chief - Story   83
Kateri Damm
Salvaged - Poem   89
Jeannette Armstrong
Ochre Lines - Poem   91
Lori New Breast
Heart Butte Dance - Poem   92
Kelly Terbasket
Nine Month Blues - Poem   93
Gunargie O'Sullivan
It's A Baby - Poem   95
Donna K. Goodleaf
Mother - Poem   100
Judy Peck
My Little Child - Poem   101

Russell Teed
Pre-Parenthood - Story   102
Anna Kruger
My Son Shine - Poem   106
Peter Blue Cloud
Grandma Marie Potts - Poem   108
Trixie Te Arama Menzies
Nga Roimata - Poem   110
Sheilia Austin
Time To Let Go - Poem   112
Jack D. Forbes
Honor Song - Poem   113
Dorothy Christian
Rebirth - Poem   119

CHILDREN

Deanna Kimball
Original Wo/man - Poem   122
Tommy Paul
The Medallion - Story   123
Kathy Joseph
Writing In Literary Forms - Poem   125
Eddie LeRoche
Rainbows and Me - Poem   126
Olivia Mercredi
I Am - Poem   127
Melissa Austin
The First Grade Five Student In Mr. Lampard's Class
To Have A (Fun) Weekend Detention - Story   128
Kevin Henry
The Beach - Story   130
Max Henry
James The Killer Whale - Story   131
Alison Austin
Flying - Poem   132
Vaughan Hedge Coke
My Favourite Place - Poem   133
Tommy Paul
Life - Poem   134
April Brass
Why Creator - Poem   135
Lawrence Angeconeb
Okijide Ikwe - Poem   136
April Stonechild
The Journey - Poem   138
Roger Van Camp
Circle of Sunlight - Poem   139

Travis Hedge Coke
Headman - Poem 140

WIND

Morningstar Mercredi
Long Wind Walk - Poem 144
Russell Teed
My Voice - Poem 146
Sharron Proulx
She Is Reading Her Blanket With Her Hands - Story 149
Carrie Jack
Mysterious Woman - Poem 155
Cheryl Ann Payne
Father I Am A woman Now - Poem 157
Cammy-Jo Mulvahill
Why? - Poem 160
Mary Lawrence
Standing At The Crossroads - Story 162
duncan mccue
Graveyard - Prose/Satire 167
Debby Keeper
Untitled - Poem 171
Janice Acoose
Where Were The Women - Poem 173
Janice Acoose
We Are Sensual/Sexual, Happy/Beautiful,
Strong/Powerful People, too - Editorial 174
Jim Logan
You're Beautiful - Poem 176
Jim Logan
Hero - Poem 177
Sarah Lyons
Sense and No Sense - Poem 178
Marcia Crosby
Speak Sm'algyax Grandma, Speak Haida Grandpa - Letter ... 180
Marie Annharte Baker
Mother In the News - Poem 185
Marie Annharte Baker
Four Directions After Her Life - Poem 186
Jeannine Peru
Ghost Rider - Story 189
Jacqueline Oker
Waiting For Welfare - Poem 195
Colin T. Jarret
Who's The Monster - Song 200
A.A. Hedge Coke
Nightmare - Story 202

Paul Ogresko
Her - Poem   205
Willow Barton
Beyond The Convent Door - Poem   206
Christopher David
They Still Talk - Poem   207
Kelly Terbasket
Chief Shining Door - Poem   208
Duncan Mercredi
Esquaw - Poem   210
Debby Keeper
How Much Longer - Poem   211
Ines Hernandez-Avila
Lemon Tea Reminds of Me of Encampments
and Velaciones - Poem   213
Morningstar Mercredi
North Wind Song - Poem   215

FIRE

Jane Inyallie
Fire - Poem   218
Gloria Roberds
Reflections Glory Days - Poem   219
Bernelda Wheeler
Reflections In A Bus Depot - Story (Exerpt)   228
Leona Hammerton
Silent Faces - Poem   234
Pauline M. Mattess
Discovering Me - Poem   235
Maxine Baptiste
Definitions - Poem   236
Richard Van Camp
The Hope of Wolves - Poem   238
Edee O'Meara
That Sage - Poem   240
Pamela Dudoward
We Three Womem - Poem   245
Richard Van Camp
My Review of "When The World Was New" - Review   248
Ines Hernandez-Avila
Canto al Parto de Sexto Sol - Poem   252
Colleen Seymour
Autumn Leaves - Poem   254
Joy Harjo
The Naming - Prose and Poem   256
Lawrence Sutherland
Meguetch Neechi - Poem   259

Willow Barton
For The Child Heart - Poem   260
Beth Cuthand
Post-Oka Kinda Woman - Poem   262
Lori New Breast
Full-Time Job - Poem   264
Colin T. Jarrett
Reach Out - Song   265
William George
Origin Stream - Poem   267

Author Biographies   271

Artist Statements   280

Acknowledgements   281

INTRODUCTION: TWO VOICES

There were disturbing signs. The trees murmured uneasily amongst themselves. Bears retreated to their caves to dream on the new dissonance percolating through their padded feet. High in the sky, winds blew back upon themselves and in the waters, deep currents rose and carved new channels in the rock shores.

And you and I are imbued in the flow of the Beginnings. The editors, the writers, and the readers align with ancient rhythms, ancient dreams. Waters of the Ancestors entreat waves to their remembrance and continuance. Mountains, bedded rock, rivers, meadows, maple, oak, alder, fir, hemlock, and cedar whisper, "Mother".

The women knew. Their timeless cycles disrupted, babies born before their time, the whispered unease of roots and medicines told them their carefully woven world was about to unravel.

In the prevailing shift of reality and our relationship with survival, we forgot. And in our seemingly forgetful state, we did not access the information. We forgot how to remember and recall the passing down of generational teachings. We forgot how to dream the original dreams to add to the newest dreams.

The birds talked. They knew. Hummingbirds flew from the southern hot lands, north and east and west, to tell the others of the carnage that scourged the nests of the human beings, and of the dark ships that churned the seas laden with the golden blood of the Mother.

Red tears bloodied, they grieved and celebrated the pain, hardship, and love of the peoples. Grounded in principles of Ancestors, soil says "Honor, respect, faith." Some heard and contributed body, heart, mind, spirit to the collective. Others were waylaid and silenced.

The white wolf howled four times and deep in the heart of the turtle, the prophets shuddered with dread. The wind came out of no place, an inexorable wind blowing contagion over the land. Millions died of disease too foreign to cure and of hearts too wounded to care. Families, tribes, nations were torn apart by the holocaust. Generations were blown into oblivion. And the survivors walked in their sleep.

Aawooo. The black wolf sang. Wolf song echoed the universe, inviting brothers and sisters to join. Gather together to sing the universe original, gather together to sing the universe anew. The bloodletting assuaged the wont of forced change. The kind of wind that slices through ribs. The fallen will be remembered; those who continue will make certain of this.

Who could reweave the colors of water, wind, earth, and fire? Who among the survivors knew the intricacies of warp and weft, pattern and weave? In the secret and sacred places, women gathered, fuelled by their fearsome love for their children and their ineluctable passion for the wild, sweet places of the heart. "We will weave the world again," they vowed.

Change in the physical, contemporary world sparks and burns with dissension and unity. With the passing down of teachings, generation to generation, we are given gifts and tools with or without knowledge of how to survive in this world. This volume of collected works challenges thinking. It invites people to fuel the spiritual nourishment in sharing voice, thoughts, and feelings that flow back to the Beginnings and remain in the present.

The web we weave is stronger than before. It must be. The colors we use are brighter. We need their light. The materials we use are as likely to be words encoded on a hard drive as they are to be oratorical words spoken with great passion in the heat of debate. We are adaptable -- we have always been.

Blues, reds, golds, greens, oranges, and indigo spiral past, present, future. Water, wind, earth, fire, women, and children connect and celebrate the circle. This edition of the _En'owkin Journal of First North American Peoples, Gatherings Volume V_ is our recognition and honor to women and children's roles in restoring the balance. The calibre of writing and art in this journal reflects the power and passion of Aboriginal writers and artists across Turtle Island and Indigenous writers and artists of the world.

Beth Cuthand and William George
Editors

Water

Christopher David

It Has Rained for a Million Years

The frog sits in council
with its ally snake

the young sit watching
with lily pad curiosity
they will learn
the importance of colored skin
in a world of patient rain

They dance water circle
life times

This will go on for a million years
then start over

The rain
teacher of the frog dance

Star Nations
for Tasina Ska Win

    I

we a nation of women
joined together
by seeds we carry
buried deep
even those of us
who have lost
have the memory
of our ancestors
our grandchildren
sewn to our souls

we together
are the stars
lighting
the blue black
we the adobe white
sky bricks
primordial
blue
the mortar
dark

we the seeds
we the stars
flowers
petals
pollen full

Odilia Galvan Rodriguez

II

look at me
I am not
a separate
woman
I am the dna
of my great grandmothers
the future
past
the present
both

we are apple
serpent red
we are moon swept
lapis oceans
full of spells

we are first life
star seeds sown
future past present known
from our blood
new ancient flowers grow

CREATION

The heart that lives
in the house of the North
burns cold as frost.
Giants sleep,
and conjurers gather,
working magic older than the earth
to gather the hoops of the sky
together over the earth
where spirits dance on frozen lakes
aurora borealis
singing dirges to travellers
on the snow.

The heart that lives
in the house of the west
born in the valley
of the shadow of death
embraces the spirits
cut loose from the bones
the mortal sticks and stones
our fathers dwelt in
in times past.

The heart that lives
in the house of the south
beats strawberry red
in frenzied cadence.
Dark fungal scent of blood
carrying spores of life
on soft warm breath
on laughing lips
in biting teeth
in clasping thighs
taut with passion
moist with the dew
of the first morning

A.Rodney Bobiwash

---

we sang into existence
when the flood waters
drained from Turtle's back
and together we closed the circle
and heard the drumming of our hearts
as one.

The heart that lives
in the house of the east
sings of the time
when the drum first spoke
and first man danced
in genesis mist
and fire-rattled sparks
from the hair of god
dropping embers,
burning holes
in the blankets between the worlds.

RESONANCE IN MOTION

In the time when they brought forth
symbols those syllable markings
indicating patterned speech The Old
Ones utilized in every spoken word
those characters translating oral tongue
without need to touch lips in our
language. In that time when Sequoia made
these available to The People enabling
those who chose to communicate
by touching ink to page, paint to
bark, by tracing design with
bent fingertip to record events.
In the time if they signed away the
mother they were put to death
by The People in accordance
with unwritten traditional law. In that
time when people of importance
showed themselves to be of
unique character. They gave their
lives to spare a friend, or relative.
When a warrior always respected
women, children, old people.
They laid down their bodies to save
The People. In the time
when all believed visions
and dreams from even the tiniest child. In
the time when honesty gave birth
to mental and spiritual freedom.
In that time we were humble,
simple as the dew on
petal tip budding fresh from
pastel pink and white dogwoods, as simple
as phases of the moon,
as simple as pass of day.
In that time we were humble,
as humble as furry
snowshoe rabbit, as young

doe with fawn internal,
as humble as The Old Ones, those turbaned
philosophers, the ones who
truly know all we can ever hope
to question. Those who are comfortable
with the flower of knowledge.
In that specific day and time,
lunar cycle, cyclic calendar.
In that ever certain movement in
time event, era span of the living and of
the dead. In that splitting fractional
second spanning up until those
foreign to this world appeared
that second in centuries of
millennium. In that time, then,
we enhanced our resonance
and place, that specific centre
of existence, we fasted,
retreated our projections
to visualize clear beyond
clarity of sight to observe
to hear the sounds resound
above, below here in this place
to understand our relation
to the skies, to those heavens
spreading every night before
and above us. Those multitudes
of lights, heavenly bodies,
seven pointed stars,
Grandmother Night Sun, the
path of the spirits
those that leave here and go
onward, those that teach
us in the singing, that vast
sky of beings united so intricately
to our own being, to the
Earth's beings, to the place
from which we come where
we find sustenance. Those

skies we follow like charts,
those suns, Mother and
Daughter, the two that
will return one day and
the one that remains for our warmth
and for the tasseled green corn to
emerge again. Sky that
holds both day and
night, light and dark,
window to the eyes of
Creator and those
spirits dwelling with him.
Even though Creator has both sides
we say Him out of respect
to our Grandfather Creator,
that giver of life, the very
point of light matching the great
peaks of earth surrounding
valleys, that giver of life Grandmother Earth
mammoth mountains her breasts, backbones,
jagged buttes, rolling hills we climbed to
pray. From these we observed to centre our-
selves. In that time we believed
that which is important which
now in this time still continues
to exist under the surface of
this world, the facade of this
time which gives us sustenance
even though we often neglect
its place of honor and importance
so significant. It allows growth
of all living beings, continuity.
Now the resonance appealing
to those with eyes of the swallow,
the openness of the innocent,
aged, infants, and little ones,
never yet jaded in humility.
This importance now in need
of blessing, of spiritual tribute

A. A. Hedge Coke

as newborn and elder
need nurturing to gift the
people with their wisdom and
renewal. Now in this time
resonance beckons nightly
in stars, in moon, in
cloudy, milky, passageway, daily in
sky, in sun,
in the masses, common man,
save the most jaded individual who
returned to a violent time in
heated latitudes. Now, in this time,
we search for what we
knew thousands of eras
ago, we bleed in quest
for those flowers. Then we
lived to a hundred and seventy-five
years and were not allowed to share
knowledge as teachers until we matured
at around fifty-two. Now
we die before we begin
approach to this span,
diseases and evils from
foreigners, our downfall. Now
pupils spring rivers cheek waterfalls
without looking to the sky
to find what appears to
be out of reach and is actually
only out of hand. Now,
in this time, we begin
again. Listen as crickets mark
these occurrences and changes
watch as sun patterns
a new depth of sky. Feel
twist in surroundings
be again. Come again to the
place from which you came to
where we do finally go, to where I beckon
you as I have been called.

A. A. Hedge Coke

It is turning. The dawn of
the next world approaching.
The generation coming.
It is turning. Do you remember
they told us. Do you remember
they brought this to us. They
directed us to live so. Do you
remember we are to always live
so as they instructed us? These
voices belong to skies, to
mountains. They belong to
past and present, they sing
future. It is in motion.

Mage is Magic

Grandmother Spider spun Her tusti bowl
and from the burning sycamore She stole
a tiny coal of fire, which She knew
could warm the very marrow of the soul.

Before the morning star arose anew
She spread Her net and caught the morning dew
in drops of sparkling jewels, every one
aquiver with each gentle breeze that blew.

The silken tapestry that She had spun
collected all the radiance of the sun
into a girasole, sunflower bright;
the fire, sun and flower shone as one.

Her woven sifter, gossamer and light
would hold a dream and put the mare to flight;
the dreams reflect a rosy aureole
to chase away the shadows of the night.

THE RUBY NECKLACE
(The Raven's Tale of the Origin of Corn)

Long ago there lived at the foothills of the mountains a Medicine Man and his wife who had two daughters. The first daughter, Dagu'ne, was frail and helpless and couldn't do much of anything. She spent most of her time looking at her reflection in the water, and brushing her long, black hair. But because she was so pretty, everybody loved her and didn't mind doing things for her.

The younger daughter, Selu'ji, was strong and healthy. She wanted to do everything all at once. She ran like a deer and climbed like a bear cub. She wandered far and wide and tasted all the wild roots and fruits and berries to see if they were good to eat. When her father saw that he was not to have any more sons, he spent more and more of his time with this younger daughter. He taught her to use the bow and arrow, to track animals, and to sing the War Songs, which was perfectly all right, because among the Cherokees a girl could grow up to be a Hunter or Warrior or a Medicine Woman or anything else she chose.

What Selu'ji liked the most was helping her father gather the wild plants that he used to cure sick people. She soon learned their names and where to find them. She found that some were to be gathered in the morning and others only when the moon was full. And most important of all, never to take all of them. "Take some and leave some," her father would say, "so that there will always be more for those who come after us."

One day an Indian Trader came by with a pack on his back. The people of the village gathered round to see what he had to offer. He opened the pack and laid out his treasures for all to see: shell necklaces from the east, turquoise rings from the west, red stone from the north, and carved jade dolls from the south, black obsidian and white ivory--little, tinkling, silver bells.

When he held up a dainty little strand of seed pearls, Dagu'ne cried out that she must have it. Her mother placed it around her neck. The price was very high, but the mother insisted that it was worth it. Her father counted out many deerskins in trade.

Dagu'ne wore her new necklace to the dance that night. Everyone came to look and told her that she was even more beautiful than the pearls. She smiled and thanked each one. She was very pleased. Her father and mother and younger sister were pleased, too.

The Trader had planned to leave at sunrise the next morning, but during the night he fell ill. The Medicine Man was called in to treat him. Selu'ji helped her father gather plants and mix them together. She watched while they simmered for hours over the fire. Everyone thought the Trader was going to die. But by the time the moon had waxed and waned, he was well again and ready to travel.

Before the Trader left, he went by to thank the Medicine Man for saving his life, and to give him a necklace of bright red beads.

The father gave the beads to Selu'ji. She could hardly believe that they were meant for her. Red was her favorite color. She could see right through each one. But how they sparkled in the sunlight! People began to notice. When they found that the stones were rubies, and very valuable, they talked of nothing else.

Dagu'ne was very jealous of her sister. Now she hated Selu'ji and all because of those silly red stones! In her anger she wanted to get rid of them. So she stole the ruby necklace and buried it in a hole at the edge of the garden.

Now the pearl necklace was the finest in the village, and Dagu'ne was happy.

Selu'ji looked everywhere for her rubies, but she never found them. She asked around, but nobody could help. It was hard to accept the loss. When she asked her sister about the mound of loose earth at the edge of the garden, Dagu'ne explained that she had planted some cattail fuzz to see if it would grow. Selu'ji kept it watered because she liked cattails.

And sure enough, several green blades pushed their way up from the top of the mound. Selu'ji watched and cared for them, but they weren't cattails at all. There was one main stalk with long green blades growing out from it. A tassel appeared at the top. Silken threads peeped out from a pocket halfway up the stalk. Later the pocket bulged and when it turned brown it cracked open. Selu'ji reached in and pulled out a hard ball that looked like a great big berry. She rubbed off some of the seeds in her hand. They were small, almost round and ruby-colored! She remembered her ruby necklace.

Could these be the lost rubies?

She called her family to come and look. Her father said he didn't know what they were. Her sister scoffed at such a fuss over some worthless seeds and threw them into the fire. In the heat of the coals, one popped and bounced back at her. The rest popped and flew in all directions.

Selu'ji picked up the nearest one and looked at it. The red seed had burst into a white bud. She smelled it. It smelled good. She tasted it. It tasted good, too.

It was popcorn. That was the first corn.

She saved half the seeds and planted them in mounds of earth as before. From these plants came corn of other colors. Grains as blue as smoke from the fire appeared along with the red ones. Then came yellow and finally white. The multi-colored ears of corn were very pretty. They were very small. They kept getting larger, and most of them turned yellow or white all over.

It was called "selu."

Selu'ji, the Corn Mother, gave to The People something far more valuable than rubies.

NOTE:
Dagu'ne is the Cherokee word for "Pearl".
Selu is the Cherokee word for "corn".
Selu'ji is the Cherokee word for "Corn Mother".

snake woman came to visit

snake woman came to visit
entered with a message
planted the old seed
of ripe change.

budding time has begun to slip
already so late
i do not notice.

beyond the reach of friends
i move into the water.
a river pulling at the bank
and out
rolling my lymied hair
straggle-weighted arm of the dredge.
lifting over stones
reason embedded
the earth dry beneath the rock

the slugs that lie there
dying with the slow coming of water
the waiwera that splits the skin.

forged in my eyes
the look of crazy snake woman
gone with the restless dance
that sheds reason
and bleeds the new-found youth
rough
on sand
and harsher labours.

intent tightens
and drawn taut
i dare the drummer's hand.

Roma Potiki

to tangi

hands cover her face
stretched plums
the colour of her fingers
holding skin

she can say nothing
not even shape the words,
only pour her hot sea
from eyes to chin.

too much has happened

anger gives
her pain the strength
to tangi
to mend its brokenness.

Karanga

Shuffling they come, the old ones long outlawed
Grey-blue their faces, their step hesitant
Trailing maidenhair hobbles them
They are aglow with phosphorescent lichen
and muddied with clay from subterranean streams

They half turn back, blinking against the glare
Watching for their companions also leaving
the dark.

These were awesome ones
Patterns on the great dark brown tree bodies
spiralling up to the incandescent eyes -
Potent the bird-men in their time.

Penetrating the earth came the broken call
which these, sure now, answer, walking towards
the blazing city of a thousand needs.

Mama God

Mama God
    the voices cry out
    Mama God
    out of your womb-mind
    the world was pulled
    sobbing
    its first breath.

Mary Isis
    they say is the Mother of God
    who then is the Father of God?
    and the Catholics pray
    with their beads
    "Holy Mary, Mother of God..."

Tonantzin
    our Holy Mother
    virgin of Tepeyac
    of Guadalupe
    speaker of Nahuatl
    Holy Earth Mother
    Daughter of Mama God
    Daughter of Papa God.

And the Mexicans say
    Our Grandparent
    the first One
    Ometeotl
    the Two-in-One Spirit
    Male and Female
    all in One
    who creates
    out of the Original Mind

the Mother Teotl
the Father Teotl

> Ometeotl
> the two-in-one
> everywhere
> Invisible Night Wind-Breath
> in everything
> but no-thing it is
> and Lame Deer's teacher said:
> the Great Spirit is not a man
> like the Christian God
> it is a power
> it could be in a cup of coffee.

Huehueteotl
> the Old One
> the Fire
> in the center
> of all being
> the breath
> the heat
> Mama-Papa
> Abuelo-Abuela
> El Viejo-La Vieja
> Now we know them
> the Mother of God
> the Father of God.

k. damm

true rock woman

you cast a long shadow
across snow-covered terrain
ice-filled moon lit lakes
past fields of wild strawberries
and the bones of grandparents a thousand years old

you cast a long shadow
across my thoughts
lending shade in days of sun-hot argument
reminding me of who i have been
and the comforting permanence of change

you cast a long shadow
through the blistering skin of my oppression
cooling the shame that burns at my cheeks
slaking the anger that scatters my freedom to the winds
easing the pain of eyes gone blind from staring at the sun

you cast a long shadow
around my soul
fill me with fear and love
terrorizing my doubt-filled inhumanity
with stone-sharp scrapings on my skull
and the threat of a living touch
unbound by false morality

you cast a long shadow
over my dreams
replacing them each morning with
the solid ground of your presence

true rock woman
you give depth to the sun

moon rite

moon calls
a gathering
in the southern
midnight sky

clouds drift in
swollen with
phosphorescent bellies
dripping the sweat
of imminent labour

waves
shift
and
stretch
wet
luminescent
skin

moans
roll
to
thunder

fluid bursts
down to earth
in torrents of
warm
embryonic
rain

Jean Wasegijig

SEARCHING

Had a dream one night,
Of sitting on a mountain ledge
Overlooking a green green valley
Down far below, a stream
Under birch and evergreens
Across more mountains
Line the valley, misty
From the morning light.

Soon after there I was
Sitting on a precipice
Words come to me
From somewhere
New phrases, different from
The Catholic schools
Or churches where I've gone.

A whisper, my name
Wakes me, my muscles tense,
Drifting off to sleep again
The wind breathes by
Leaves lift and tumble
And cover me gently
As if I am one of them.

RISING SUN WOMAN

Rising Sun Woman paddles down the river
Water glistening on her paddle
Black hair shining in the morning sun;
Gentle swish and gurgle of paddle
Says
Rising Sun Woman is coming,
Says
Rising Sun Woman is coming
to
Birds of the morning.
Young Morning Breeze
Kisses
Rising Sun Woman on cheeks-lips-throat
Morning Breeze
Says
Rising Sun Woman is coming,
Rising Sun Woman is coming.
And
Rising Sun Woman paddles down the river
Water glistening on her paddle
Black hair shining in the morning sun;
Rising Sun Woman is coming,
Coming to the
Land Where River Meets The Great Waters.
The canoe of Rising Sun Woman
is
Light but strong; it carries the
Spirit of Cedar Tree it once was.
And in her canoe
Rising Sun Woman paddles homeward
to
the Great Village of the Salmon People.
Rising Sun Woman has stories
to
Tell and Secrets to whisper to
Her people,

Valerie Dudoward

Salmon People in the Great Village.
She has been in the
Land of the Mountain Goat People
for
All the Snow Moons
but
Today
She is free in the spring air
and
Rising Sun Woman smiles and paddles down the river
Water glistening on her paddle
Black hair shining in the morning sun.

MY RAIN IS RAIN

Rain pours on the cars and the concrete
The world outside is grey and dark
This is spring in the city
And I don't like it
While a thousand miles away
The springtime of my village home
Is marked by deep puddles in the dirt road
Young buds of salmonberry bush and wild rose
Dogs and children romp through the puddles
Old men stand by the bridge smoking
Fishermen work on their engines
Women take walks together between cloudbursts
And plan their departure for seaweed camp
Their rain is a time of promise
Their rain reflects renewal
Their rain brings them together
Their rain is power
My rain is rain

Not Defeated

We watched you and I
from a distance
grandfather bent over the paper leaves
knife men with parting sticks standing by.
This day and many others I've
wanted those parting sticks pointed
hard and straight.

We were eating summer pups
buffalo heaped in sour heat
no rabbits, no berries
to fill our dying bellies.
Our warriors crying
beneath the Sundance Tree
falling from barking parted sticks.
Ghost Dancers whistling
bleeding shirts.
We were dying. We were dying.
Dying.

Grandfather talked with Grandmother.
Grandmother said
Riverblood will always be our milk.
Our fires will never die.
Grass will spring in our hearts.
This talk will stain the paper leaves.

Grandfather carried his bending
spirit and joined
the other walk-far eyes.
They shared the pipe.

This is how it came to be
Grandfather drawing suns, moons
lakes, winds and grass in his
feathered hands.

For Blankets and Trinkets

My father dreamt
our winter sleep and lifting wails
was the coming Chinook
not knowing when we traded
our furs we'd hover in bones.
He said our winters would be
pelts of thick sky
no longer weighed down
in buffalo curls.

That year the frog arrived
my heart wrapped
around the thick traders blankets.
My babies pimpled with poison.

Oh little one, I wasn't as fortunate
as your aunt. She was traded
with a man of wonder heart.
I've become a gopher
jumping hole to hole
cutting roots to keep
my teeth dull. I was crazed hunger.
my bones piercing my flesh
arms dried branches too weak
to bury my speckled babies.
My heart, a gooseberry
rolling past my tongue.

I went with the man
with a wooden tail
his grunting and guttural tongue
a grizzly that eats my breast.
I am parched grass
satisfying my thirst
with spirits hidden in his water.
My dance frozen in my feet.
My father's wails long
buried in winter sleep.

Beth Cuthand

This Red Moon
For Steven with love

Tonight
the moon is a hard red disk.

Passpassces predicted it would be so.

Your Grandpa told me the old man
fasted for twelve days
with my Great-Grandfather, Missatimos
at Manito Lake
in the time of the
hungry pup when the people
were starving and fearful
of what lay ahead.

Passpassces dreamed far and saw many things.

"The people shall suffer a long war," he said.

Passpassces saw and knew
in this red moon
flowed the blood of memories;

> groping hands in the night,
> innocent children crying silent
> keeping secrets too fearful
> to tell. Too shamed to know
>
> it was not their fault.
>
> black whirlwinds raging anger
> turned back inside our souls
> men beating women, the
> mirrored images of their own self-hate

children watching
>   thinking terror is life
>   and love too   bloody to risk.

Passpassces saw the black water
invading our sacred spaces,
drowning our knowing that
life is to be lived and
love is what heals

Our relations cried out for us
in their love in their love
for our red clay blood
cradled in our land covered in sky.

In that dark night they called
creation to guide us.
and
they smoked together and prayed.

Passpassces held the pipe
and wept and shivered for
the ache of our starving
and the confusion of memory
hardened to shame.

>   "The red moon tells us
>   The way back to life will be
>   by doing battle inside ourselves.
>
>   This will not be war as we have known it:
>   Many will die in the fight
>   Many will run from the blood letting
>   Many will hide in the black water
>   Many will try to escape by the color of their skin

But

>   More will claim their warrior blood
>   More will pray their road to peace

Beth Cuthand

    More will dance under the thunderers' nest
    More will sing their way to freedom
    More will make their marks on paper
    in the spirit telling of all this
    that we pray for those not yet born."

Passpassces fell silent
and the people murmured amongst themselves
fearful for our future
not knowing if we would find the courage
nor even recognize the war

"How will we survive?" they cried
(meaning all of us for seven generations to come)

How will we survive?

There's no way forward
but through
this red moon blood of memory
and the telling of it son.

And the victory

And the victory.

THE MOON IS OUR MESSENGER

tonight i am inside the moon
and she is full & smiling

she is my mother, my friend
my lover, my sister
we embrace each other, become part of each other
she nurtures me with her soft solar heat
and illuminating midnight shine

sister
when i heard about your pain
i cried
i wanted to be there with you
to help you
i wanted to nurture you
and give you warmth
some of my shine

when i heard about your pain
i asked the sun
why?
why make her suffer
she who means so well
sharing herself with others
she who works so hard
giving herself to others
she who helps us to understand
why the sun moves inside the moon at night
and the light of a thousand hopes
becomes one solid circle in the sky

tonight
while the moon is full
i think of you
hoping life finds you healing now

Victoria Lena Manyarrows

the moon is our messenger
the darkness our guide
those distant sparkles called stars
are our eyes
glimmering thru the faint haze
embracing this city

i gaze at you in the moon
her face is your face
and you are smiling

i think of you and hold you close
sending you well wishes, healing spirits
thru the darkness
to your ever-shining moon

WERE YOU THERE?

Ceremony.
Full circle.
Left to right.

Enter
with appropriate dress.
Come as you are.
Hear the stories,
before our time.
Later,
I hope.

Determined knees.
Untrained outstretched legs.

Blankets of life,
wait
to comfort you
for the hours to come.

The moon shaped altar
with its road of life,
appears so short.

In here one can experience
how precious life is...
Grasp some meanings
of reality.

The charcoal scorches.
Is it the flint?
The firekeeper,
rakes over the body

The body
shows many
figures, faces, symbols...

Colleen Seymour

The body becomes
uncomfortably hot.

The square cut corn husks,
are chosen, licked, loaded, and rolled.
The smoke is lit
from a light passed on
by the firekeeper.
It is remembered
that the smoke
must be kept at a forty-degree angle.
The taste to lips is pleasantly different.

The exhaled smoke rises,
soon evaporates
not to nothingness,
but to the Creator.

The Creator is present
he hears
the prayers
of the night
even all at once.

How many times
in different places,
different situations,
were similar feats
prayed for
so that a connection
could happen?

Tonight,
the instrument people,
who have been a part
of this ceremony
from the beginning
are now honored.
decorated in their finery

they are blessed
by the poor man.

People are
minuscule particles here.

Think of it!
Have you ever been able to
count each snowflake
as it reached
to blanket the earth?

Each one is a body.
Its life is shorter than a human life.
If enough snowflakes gather
in one place
things can start to happen.
Beauty by no contrast,
or
destruction.

Oh, Precious Prince of Peace
We simpletons need assistance.
Our people
are falling around us like short lived snowflakes.
They too have
stories
beautiful
yet destructive.

Ceremony.
Full circle.
Left to right.
Tonight the tea,
the sacred medicine
is passed.

The person at the head of the altar,
the poor man

Colleen Seymour

speaks.
Anyone at anytime
may roll a smoke
or consume the medicine.

Once we were
blessed with
corn pollen,
once cedar was burned.
Once
happened many times
though.

As the moon
changed places in the sky,
that night
the instrument boxes waited,
waited for the
midnight call for water.
And the blowing
of the
eagle bone whistle
called sky to earth.

Then and only then
were the boxes opened.
Magic could happen
with belief.
Even though believing
is so hard
for ribbed-boned bodies.

This is
the moment.
Let the ceremony
Begin.
Full circle.
Left to right.

Those Things That Come to You at Night

"Old Woman, Grandmother," she said. "They come to me at night."
"What is it they want?"
"Can't tell. Ain't like I really hear them clear."

Like voices I've known
sounding off
over the hill
behind the milk shed
under the belly of a car
coming through the woods
familiar tones and rhythms
like surface conversation
heard while underwater
the sliding pitch of sound
but no clear word borders.

"You must try to hear and remember. Sounds, pictures, the stories they bring you, the songs."

Swimming among the fluid notions
of dream space
where voices land
in the hollow behind the house
and echo back to sleeping souls
where ideas ricochet
off of each documented waking moment
but strike home
in the slumbering core.

"They tell me things I'm sure. I want to get up to follow. But I can't pull my body along. When I wake up I am homesick for those voices. And then sometimes, maybe when I am hauling water or frying bacon, I remember something, just a feeling really."

The old woman, bent over her basket, nods her head slowly. "Yes," she says. The younger one waits. Nothing more.
Night speaking
touching spirit
without distinguishable words or voice
calling by name

Kimberly Blaeser

calling your ancient being
arousing that felt destiny
walking all past
folding the torn moments together
and shaking them out whole.

"Grandmother?"
"It's that way, child. The night things. Like how you learned to walk. Nobody can teach you."

Now a rumbling comes
heard over a heartbeat
beating more rapidly
with a fear of
greatness
felt in the bladder
breathed with flared nostrils
approaching like a flood
it rushes upon you
cleanses you with night desire
leaves you floating peacefully
into daylight.

"They get louder, I'm told."
"The voices?"
"Ayah. Louder if you don't seem to hear. Louder still until you hear or go deaf. Everybody has a choice you know. Some go night deaf. Others learn to listen."

Singing the songs
of midnight
going quiet, smiling shyly
when someone hears
listening inside
voices rounding each corner
of yourself
forming you
from daylight
remembering
those things
that come to you at night.

Stars, Tadpoles And Water

as a youth I often wondered
why everything needed a specific name
why a star swimming in the dark night sky
was not a tadpole swimming in water on the earth?

to understand that Crow is the keeper of knowledge is to say
a great many people would gasp and prefer the square hole
although they are by all outward appearances round peg legs
in the cycle of life-long yearning/learning to adjust
to the noise of falling rocket ships and dreams overhead
at the stock exchange at the bus stop shuffling their feet
in the unemployment line waiting for the highly esteemed
over priced politician to amputate what remains of hope
submerged beneath the junk pile of things to do places to be

        actions reactions
        and all these things

running together as they often do held prisoner by
chain smoking alcohol aspirin dope the next morning cancer and aids
to prove how much we are dis-connected one from the other
from the tribe from the earth from water from touching
feeling the familiar roots of a familiar place familiar faces
in the clouds roll along day upon day in the sky of your dreams
in the mud puddle of real life after a refreshing spring rain
reflecting the birth and movement of Stars and Tadpoles

itself a reflection of other worlds too quick for the eyes

other times

in other words
the bone laden fossil stones collected with a living pinch of
tobacco at the creek bed left by moving mountains of water
in the long ago teach tell us that our lives are not permanent
indentations on the sacred water sacred circle sacred red path

Blue Heron/ Jose Garza

---

water decides wind decides earth decides sun decides how
each symmetrical duplication of the pattern of the body of each
living thing frozen in time has returned to the hard stone
reality that life escapes is gathered back by forever moving
rivers of changing energy each in their own time wordless timeless
each by their own ice age moved
a whirling fire storm unexpected

to understand that plants and trees share secrets among themselves
communicate their eating habits feel pain rejoice at the onset
of the new spring rains is to know that life is fragile just ask
the dinosaurs who thought nothing of chasing the others around
tearing apart the vegetation plotting the conquest of the world
by sheer numbers and force of arms legs and sharp jaws unaware
of the immense power of our Mother to straighten Herself out
when the asteroid weight of the fiery monsters became too great

Just ask the Full Moon
    ask the Old Ones waiting
    ask the Water you drink everyday
    ask the child with Starshine in her eyes

Contributions By Choctaw Women To The Study Of Choctaw History

Few European or American observers have ever become well enough acquainted with the inner workings of Choctaw culture to appreciate the powerful role of women in Choctaw traditional life. Blinded by their own patriarchy, the colonizers have been slow to appreciate that Choctaw culture is matrilineal and in many respects matriarchal.

For nearly two hundred years, at least since the arrival of evangelical Christian missionaries in the Choctaw country in 1818, Americans have attempted to impose their culture, their religion, and their patriarchy upon the Choctaws. Choctaws have adjusted to the expectations of the colonizers in many visible positions of leadership, especially political roles, but in Choctaw traditional life, especially family life, and also including many organizations, a mature female will be found at the very center of the group, whether particularly visible to outsiders or not.

For endeavours depending upon individual initiative, unfettered by the shackles of a foreign-imposed patriarchy, there may be no better example of the natural grace with which Choctaw women assume leadership roles than in the field of professional historians. Among the Eurocentrics, it is a field long dominated by men. Among the Choctaw it is a field dominated by Choctaw women.

In the second and third quarters of the twentieth century, two pioneer Choctaw women historians, Muriel Wright and Anna Lewis, set a high standard for others to follow. Both were descended from distinguished Choctaw families.

Muriel Wright was the granddaughter of Allen Wright, who was Principal Chief of the Choctaw Nation from 1866 to 1870, and she was the daughter of Dr. Eliphalet Nott Wright, a physician and surgeon who was a graduate of Albany Medical College, Albany, New York. Muriel Wright was born in the Choctaw Nation in 1889. In 1905, she was sent to Massachusetts to be educated at the Wheaton College, a school for women. From 1908 to 1910 she was privately tutored in Washington, DC, and spent much of her time in the Library of Congress and the Smithsonian Institution, while her father served as resident Choctaw delegate to the United States government. In the fall of 1911, she was admitted as a senior to East Central State College, in Ada, Oklahoma, and graduated the following spring. She later received graduate instruction in History and English at Barnard College, the women's unit of Columbia University in New York City, until World War I interrupted her studies.

Throughout the 1920's and 1930's, she produced a remarkable body of scholarship, mostly in topics of Choctaw history, consisting of sixteen major articles in *The Chronicles Of Oklahoma*, the quarterly scholarly journal of the Oklahoma Historical Society, but also including two textbooks on Oklahoma history and a third one which she co-authored. From 1943 to 1955 she served as associate editor of *The Chronicals Of Oklahoma*, and from 1955 to 1973 as editor.

When she retired in 1973, she had published a total of ninety-five journal articles and twenty-nine book reviews in *The Chronicles Of Oklahoma*, had authored or co authored seven books, and compiled or edited six others. Her magnum opus, *A Guide To The Indian Tribes Of Oklahoma* (University of Oklahoma Press, 1951), is a monumental work that will never lose its value. Her distingushed career brought her honors from many state, national, and international organizations, including in 1940, induction into the Oklahoma Hall of Fame, and, in 1964, the award of an honorary Doctor of Humanities degree by Oklahoma City University. In 1971, the North American Indian Women's Association honored her as "the outstanding Indian Woman of the Twentieth Century."

As Muriel Wright was a dedicated scholar and editor, Anna Lewis was a dedicated scholar and teacher. Born in the Choctaw Nation in 1855, descendant of the prominant Lewis family, she graduated from the Choctaw Nation's Tushkahoma Female Institution in 1903. She received further instruction at Mary Conor Junior College in Paris, Texas, and at Jones Academy in the Choctaw Nation before receiving the B.A. degree in 1915 and M.A. degree in 1918 from the University of California at Berkeley. In 1930, she became the first woman to receive the Doctor of Philosophy degree from the University of Oklahoma.

All her life a teacher, Anna Lewis began her career in teaching at two Choctaw national schools in the Choctaw Nation. After statehood, she taught at Bokchito and in the Durant City schools. In 1916 she taught at Oklahoma Presbyterian College, and in 1917 she joined the faculty at the Oklahoma College for Women. There she became head of the Department of History and held that position until her retirement in 1956.

Her doctoral dissertation was published in 1932 under the title *Along The Arkansas,* (Southwest Press), a study of 18th century French-Indian relations along the lower Arkansas River valley. Throughout her life she contributed journal articles to *The Chronicles of Oklahoma, The Arkansas Historical Quarterly, The Mississippi Valley Historical Review,* and publications of the University of California Press, and she was a contributor to the *Dictionary of American Biography* and the *Encyclopedia Britannica.*

Her life's work, however, a labor of twenty years, is entitled *Chief Pushmataha--American Patriot: The Story of the Choctaws' Struggle for Survival* (Exposition Press, 1960), which she painstakingly researched in the University of California's Bancroft Library, the University of Oklahoma, the State Library of Mississippi, and the Library of Congress. Despite its title, the book is anything but a work of American patriotism, and, in addition to being the definitive biography of the great Okla Hannali Choctaw war chief, is a straightforward recitation of the betrayal of the Choctaw people by the government of the United States. When she completed the manuscript, in the 1950's, during one of the most intellectually repressive periods in American history, she found that no press would publish it. Among the book's original contributions, she discovered in the State Department files that Andrew Jackson had secured the signature of Okla Falaya Choctaw Chief Puckshennubbe to the treaty of 1820 by means of blackmail. Puckshennubbe's daughter married an American soldier, who had deserted; Jackson learned of this and threatened to have Puckshennubbe's son-in-law shot if the chief did not sign the treaty. In the midst of the McCarthy era of the 1950's, Anna Lewis could find no press bold enough to publish her book. Finally, in failing health, just a year before she died, to the undying gratitude of all future generations of Choctaws, she borrowed money from her sister and paid to have the book published by a vanity press in New York City. Why, in the years since, no university press has reprinted her book is a source of great mystery to the Choctaws.

Like Muriel Wright, Anna Lewis received many honors during her life, including, also in 1940, induction into the Oklahoma Hall of Fame. In 1930, she was named one of the twenty-four prominent women of Oklahoma, in *Who's Who,* later in *Women in Who's Who* and *Who's Who In Oklahoma*. She was a founder of the Oklahoma chapter of Delta Kappa Gamma, a national honorary teachers' society.

It might be noted here that non-Native women have also made great contributions to the study of Choctaw history, perhaps inspired by the examples of two great ladies of Choctaw history. Angie Debo, a premiere historian of American Indian history, wrote her doctoral dissertation on a topic of Choctaw history at the University of Oklahoma in 1934, published by the University of Oklahoma Press as *The Rise And Fall Of Choctaw Republic*. Ruth Tennison West, after receiving her M.A. in History at the University of Texas, devoted ten years of her life to an exhaustive study, published in the summer of 1959 in *The Chronicles Of Oklahoma* and titled 'Pushmataha's Travels.' Women, both Native and non-Native, seem drawn to the study of Choctaw history, and they have clearly established themselves as the leaders in the field. Many other names could be listed: Mary Elizabeth Young, Thelma Bounds, Laura Edna Baum, Pamelia Coe, Natalie Morrison Denison, Myrtle Drain, Etha M. Langford, Frances Densmore, Emma Lan Lea, Betty C. Ridley, Armita S. Spaulding, Barbara G. Spencer, Vera Alice Toler, Dorothy Milligan, Allene DeShazo Smith, Patricia Dillion Woods, Patricia Galloway, Carolyn Keller Reeves, to mention but a few.

Today, Choctaw women continue the tradition of leadership in this field. In 1980 Clara Sue Kidwell, formerly of the University of California at Berkeley, now at the Smithsonian Institution, co-authored the invaluable study titled *The Choctaws: A Critical Bibliography* (University of Illinois Press for the Newberry Library). Kidwell's latest work, still a work in progress, is tentatively titled *They Stack Them On The Ramparts*, a study of early Christian missionary activity among the Choctaws. In 1986, Roseanna Tubby co-authored *After Removal: The Choctaw In Mississippi* (University of Mississippi Press). In 1992, Scott Kayla Morrison and LeAnne Howe published *Sewage of Foreigners* in Federal Bar Journal and Notes, a courageous work of investigative journalism concerning contract negotiations to turn Mississippi Choctaw land into a dumping ground for toxic waste, a work which is now under contract with the University of Oklahoma Press to be expanded into a book. When these Choctaw women write, they are following a tradition pioneered earlier in this century by Choctaw women like Muriel Wright and Anna Lewis, but when they move naturally and gracefully to speak their minds, they are also following a tradition among Choctaws as old as time.

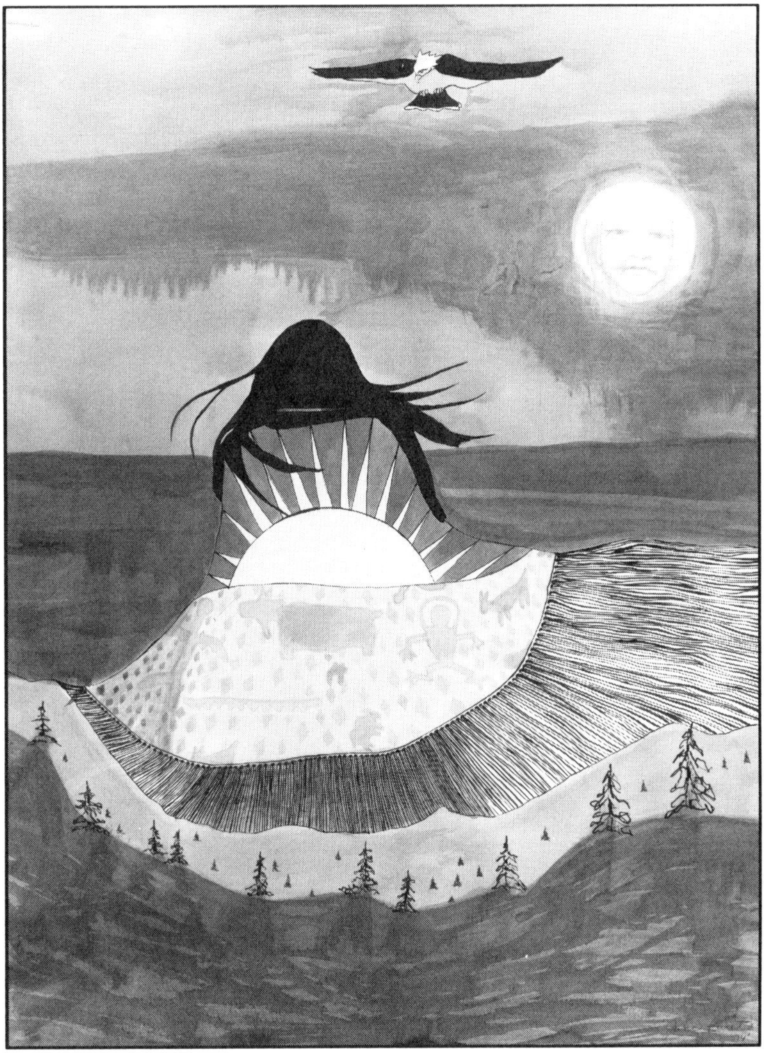

Earth

Victoria Lena Manyarrows

AMERICA/LOVE SONG TO THE NATIVE LANDS

since yesterday
    i've wanted you
dreaming of soft grasses
    blowing in the wind
velvet-soft hills rising
high
valleys dipping low

i've dreamed of your wetlands
    drenched by storms & dripping
wet, so wet
waterfalls cascading, rivers racing
tropical whirlwinds bringing many pleasures
    flowers florescent
    lush growth iridescent
    wild birds singing
    waters welcoming
    new beginnings

i've dreamed of travelling deep into your canyons
where streams meander quietly & cliffs reach high
fissures separating
caverns opening
deep into your copper canyons
scarlet sunsets
thirsting desert lands

i've dreamed of travelling deep into your fiery center
past steaming geysers
boiling springs
volcanic overflows
i've dreamed of lying together with you on your lava beds
and feeling your heat unending

i've dreamed of travelling to where your heart's a searing blaze
> *unrelenting*

america
> *my native land*
will you ever know how much i love you?

Peter Blue Cloud/Aroniawenrate

Autumn Morning

Full moon and the whispering leaves
of dry corn stalks touched by wind
a low mist swirls the river's surface
in gentle dance, like visions lent
by starlight the owl's eyes reflect,
and moon path on water is a walking
murmur of soft questions
      only a child will ask.
And maple's shadow is a pattern
woven by Creation in balance
of earth and sky,
      then softly
again the owl's call, an inner
sound of warm feathers,
then sudden gust of wind
announces day with a shower
of falling leaves which dance
a frantic, short-lived race.
      And dawn is a praise of silence
      to be respected.

She
sings
us
sweetly,
touches
our
feet
with
dance,
hands
us
golden
fruit,
hums
us
night
songs
we
ever
taste.

THE OGOPOGO
To Lynn, who believes.

Ogopogo:
a large marine animal of unknown origin said to inhabit the Okanagan Lake in the Canadian province of British Columbia. The Ogopogo has many parallels to the Loch Ness creature in Scotland.

1

Fencing is slow, methodical work, and I was glad for the excuse of my sister's visit. I took off my hat to wipe the sweat from my face and waited as Lillian hurried towards me, a storm of kids swarming around her. Behind her the lake cast a perfect mirror reflection of the low hills. On the other side, a mile away, a single blue motor boat plowed along the shoreline, a distant drone of annoyance in an otherwise peaceful world.

The kids reached me first, most of them trailing towels and assorted clothing with them from the beach. Lillian was yelling, "You've got to see...bigger than...my Uncle said that...pogos don't look you..." Lillian's excitement was contagious, which explained why the kids were so noisy. I couldn't make out what they were trying to say. My sister's black eyes were round and her shoulders were shaking.

"I'm sorry. I can't hear you," I yelled at her, and I gave up as the small hurricane of activity swept around me. Lil suddenly sat down, hard, onto the ground. The kids swarmed around me and then, in a trail of dust and sound, were gone, dashing up the dirt road towards the distant houses..

"Sis, you okay?" I asked. Lil looked up from the ground and swallowed.

"Sis, what's wrong? Is it the kids? Were they too much?"

Lil shook her head and again swallowed, trying to speak.

"If it's Ralph acting up again, I'll speak to his mom. That boy has to learn some manners. Always going and coming like he does, it's enough to..."

"Shut up! Will you shut up! You're as bad as the kids."
I moved half a step back from the force of her voice. Lil reached up,

grabbing my left arm for support as she pulled herself to a standing position with a grunt of effort. Her long braided hair was made blacker by the sun's brightness, so black that I could see the bluish tinge that glinted when her hair caught the light in a certain way. Lil stood there staring at me.

"Well, what is it?" she demanded.
"What is what?"

"How come you're staring at me like that?"

"I wasn't staring. I was just looking at your hair."

Lil reached up and smoothed down the top of her hair. She half-turned her head to look at one of her braids. The next thing I knew she was staring up the road at the receding whirlwind of dust. Her right hand shielded her eyes from the sun but even so she squinted.

"Where are those damn kids going?"

"Probably up to the house. You were saying something before you fell."

"I didn't fall." Again, Lil glared at me with those dark eyes, daring me to say anything to the contrary. I knew better, and remained silent, twisting the rim of my hat in both hands.

"Hmph! If you were listening, you'd have heard what I was trying to tell you. There's something down by the lake. Something big. I think it's the Ogopogo."

I must have been staring blankly at Lil because she went and kicked me in the shins.

"Hey! What'd you do that for?"

"Ah, you asked for it. Don't you believe me?"

I thought better of reminding my dear sister about the time six months ago when she'd seen a flying saucer near the garbage dump by the reserve. She still had a hard time living that one down. Humour her, I thought.

"Okay, so what's the gag?"
"It ain't no gag. I tell you, I saw something down by the lake. It darned near scared the shit out of the kids who were swimming."

I played along. "Okay, sis, how big was it?"

Lil's eyes became round again. "Big! It was really big."

She must have seen my eyes glaze over because the next thing I knew she'd tied into me and I was staring up at her.

"Get up! Get up and I"ll show you. I"ll bet you don't dare come down and see."

I was getting up when I saw the distant dust storm of kids once more heading our way. Only this time it'd grown. There was no use fighting the inevitable. I nodded and Lil led the way back down to the lake's edge. A single frail pier jutted some hundred feet onto the lake. There was no wind and the waters were still as a mirror. I could see several small white clouds reflected in the lake's stillness. The power boat had moored somewhere unseen, leaving the entire lake empty of movement. I stared the length and breadth of the lake for as far as I could see but there was nothing but water.

Lil stood by my side, a look of triumph on her face.

"There. You see. I told you so."

I was missing something here.
"What am I supposed to be looking for?"

Lil gave a snort of sheer disgust just as the whirlwind of kids stormed up to us. Several adults had joined them and for the next five minutes people were yelling at each other and pointing to the lake. I continued to stare at the water but there wasn't a sign of movement. The voices of the kids dominated everything.

"...a giant beaver that got lost in..."

"...Dad said...this big, maybe bigger, and..."

"...sturgeons at least a hundred years old were..."

"...ain't nothin' but your imag..."

"...close to it I could almost touch it..."

I finally turned to Lil, trying to ignore the kids yelling at each other and at the adults.

"So what did you see?" I yelled.

Lil pointed at the waters. "It was over there, about a hundred feet out. And it was big. As big as a whale, maybe bigger."

Having no idea how big whales were, I stared at the spot where she was pointing. Nothing. No matter how hard I stared there was nothing.

Lil saw my baffled look and pointed again. "I swear, it was there. Geoff," and here Lil pointed at one of the yelling boys. "Geoff was the closest. It almost hit him and he panicked."

"Sis, where were you?"

"I was laying on my blanket. I heard the yelling and turned to see the kids running for shore. I could see at least two humps behind them. The thing was dark so I couldn't make out what it really looked like. And it was moving fast."

I stared at the water, my eyes hurting from the want. And then a shadow moved under the water a hundred feet from shore. A long dark shadow which twisted towards the surface as Lil screamed and turned to run.

"Wait," I yelled, but it was too late. A torrent of people poured up the dry road towards the safety of their homes. I took a last look at the shadow and saw a second shadow, longer and thinner, below that of the first. The first shadow broke the surface of the water and I saw the single broken branch rise in the air from the lower part of the trunk. Disgusted, I turned to follow the clouds of dust.

That night I heard the stories around the campfire. Excitement filled the voices of each speaker, some of them elders. It seemed half the reserve was down on the beach, but nothing was found. Of course, not many boats travelled too far from the beach and the lights. I told my story, but I was careful not to fuel the imaginations of the kids. They'd be up half the night as it was. Nor did I mention the branch I'd seen on the trunk of the old tree.

A week later I'd almost forgotten the whole thing when I happened to pick up the daily newspaper and read the bold headlines. Here we go again, I thought. The story mentioned the sighting. My sister's story was featured as were the scattered quotes from some of the children who'd been there that day.

I was about to skip to the sports section when a single paragraph near the end of the article caught my eye. A man who owned a small blue boat said he'd seen the group of Indians on the other side of the lake. He'd crossed over, saw the shadow and followed it until he'd caught up with it. He claimed that it was just a tree trunk caught in a riptide. Nothing more would have come of it except that the man swore that as he pulled the tree to shore he saw another shadow, deeper in the water, follow his boat's trail for a good quarter mile before it sank out of sight. That shadow had been longer and narrower.

Is there an Ogopogo? I don't know, but I no longer turn off my sister when she starts speaking about it. Now I'll never really know.

2

The feast was going well. Some two hundred people were seated in the hall, filling it with a low hum. Very formal, very boring. I bolted down my food, trying to finish as fast as I could so I could make a quick run for the door and freedom. Tomorrow I was going deer hunting and I needed my rest.

"Hey, Martha, there's Joe. You know, the one who saw the Ogopogo."

I looked up in a panic. Several people nearby turned to stare at me and I looked down at my plate. The emcee swept by and I hunched down in my seat, trying not to draw any notice. The single slice of fried bread and the almost empty cup of coffee were the last things in front of me. A minute and I'd be out of here. I was doing this only for my sister, Lillian. I hated crowds.

The emcee reached the stage where he fumbled with the mike, tapping it gently. The dull thumps echoed through the hall and conversations dropped as people, including those near me, turned their attention to the stage.

The fried bread tasted so good that I chewed a couple extra times rather than simply swallowing.

"Thank you, ladies and gentlemen, for coming to our annual feast and fund raiser. I hope you all enjoyed the meal? Well, did you?"

A wave of applause broke out, and I joined in rather than finishing off my coffee.

The emcee smiled, clearly enjoying his job. The applause died down and I reached for my coffee.

"Tonight we're going to have entertainment for you all. We scheduled a dance to begin the ceremonies, but on the way up here I noticed Joe."

It wasn't fair. Give me five more seconds, please.
"You all know Joe, don't you?" The emcee smiled and pointed at me. Everyone turned and I sucked in my breath feeling the whole world stop. I knew people could see the blood rushing to my face.

"Stand up, Joe. Joe and his sister Lillian saw the Ogopogo last month. You all remember that, don't you? It was in the papers. Come on up here, Joe, and tell us about it."

As everyone clapped I felt something pull me to my feet. The something turned out to be my sister, who was in her glory as she waved to the audience. "Get up there, and don't make idiots of us," she whispered to me.

Before I could protest, she pushed me towards the front of the stage. It was worse than "Aliens." The walk to the stage seemed to last forever, and by the time I got to the mike I was soaked with sweat. In ceremonies no one can hear you scream.

I stared at the audience, who stared back. There wasn't a sound in the hall, and I felt like Sigourney Weaver. Any moment the audience would turn into creatures ready to suck my face off. I was defenseless. Remember the crewman they always beamed down with Captain Kirk and Spock on "Star Trek"? You always knew the poor sap was going to bite the bullet. Dog meat. Chopped liver.

I kept staring at the audience and they kept staring back. The seconds turned into minutes which turned into hours, and they just stared at me, not making a sound. I was losing pounds of sweat every second and they just stared at me, waiting for me to crack, which I did, of course.

I smiled, my eyes big as dinner plates, and I slowly took the mike in my hands. Still watching the audience, I pulled the mike closer to my face and then I bit into it.

The next thing I knew I was staring at the ceiling. Everything hurt, even my hair, which stood straight up, what there was of it. My sister's face was among those who looked down at me. I must have looked like a demented chihuahua on steroids. As they carried me out amid the ensuing bedlam, the last words I heard were from the emcee.

"Give Joe a hand, folks. What an act! What a card! I told you he'd be great."

THE END

Odilia Galvan Rodriguez

Widow's Clothes
for my son Hawk

when the light in his eyes for me went out
you were just a newborn baby boy
and like my grandmothers long ago
who lost their husbands young
I chose my widow's clothes   have been in them ever since

in the seven years I have been
clutching you close to my breasts
you have never seen me love another
emanating from my clothes   the grays and blacks
all you've smelled is the cedar from the chest where   I locked my
heart away

I love you blue rivers and grand canyons deep
it is not like that big love I put down to sleep
but rather the love of a mother for her son
a love that started from the quickening of your life in my red womb
is with us both   all our lives   then forever after on the other side

how do I tell you now
explain this kind of love   I had forgotten myself
did not believe would ever come to me again
having accepted loneliness   it took a miracle to help me see
there can be love after the sifting of the grey and black ashes of
mourning is through

all I can say is   the perfume you smell now
seeping from my pastel dress   is from a field of wild flowers
and jewelled hummingbirds nest   in that place that I had locked
up dark and tight
waiting content for that perfect spring day   when they will try
their new wings
when they will buzz away sweetly   into the turquoise sky

SURVIVAL

I see a shadowface
in the trees....
I lean against
the ancient, wrinkled bark
dried and lined thru time
aging with the majestic grace
of an elder and
I feel it's strength.

Roots embedded deep
beneath warm, moist earth
holding on
to the will to survive
searching for sustenance
to replenish its limbs
that it may grow
branches reaching high
to bear seed
and re-forest its image
...as the cold steel claws
tear at the Earth.

I lean against this tree
arms encircled
holding on
to the shadowface
of my ancestors
etched in a thousand years.

Henry Michel

Paved Memory

Jane looked through Grandma's old trunk that she inherited from her mom. She had used it as an ornament for years without surveying its contents. Glancing at the couch, she saw that Sally, her sixteen month old baby, still slept soundly. It seemed that Sally had been sleeping for such a long time. Jane was surprised to find that only fifteen minutes had passed since she opened Grandma's trunk.

Jane leafed through her Grandma's pictures. Each picture touched different emotions inside her. Both her parents, and all of her Aunts and Uncles, were gone. She wondered how they would feel about their children's lives if they were still here. She wondered if they would be satisfied with the way she lived her life and how she raised her child. Once again she glanced over at Sally. For a moment she imagined that her Aunt Annie was standing there, looking over Sally as well.

Jane remembered her Aunt Annie's warm presence. Aunt Annie had always been at Granny's whenever she visited. Auntie always took the time to do special little things for her. Jane enjoyed how Auntie fixed her hair and found little colourful things to put in it. Her aunt always told her to be real good to herself. She explained, "You have to be your best whenever you go to someone's house. Even when going to school, take the time to look your best." Jane missed that attention.

Jane looked at Sally and wondered if she was taking the time for her baby like her aunt would have liked. She wondered whether she was taking the time for herself. The thought that she didn't have family here in the city since she moved two years ago troubled her. Suddenly she felt so alone. She had seen none of her relatives for months. She remembered the times she spent with Grandma and the times Aunt Jane and Uncle Bill visited their home - there were always people around. Now Sally and she spent weeks at a time alone. Rob never seemed to be around any more. He was always out working or running around for his relatives, and they never seemed to visit lately.

Jane had married Rob six years before. Neither of them drank now, and Rob was a good provider for her and Sally, always attentive and affectionate to them. Jane convinced herself that she didn't have anything to complain about. She decided to get back to her daily chores. Just then, Sally stirred.

Jane picked up Sally and brought her back to Grandma's trunk. She wondered why she was going through Grandma's things. She had kept the trunk since her mother died, never paying much attention to it. Sally shook one of Grandma's boxes, which had been collecting dust, in the corner of the trunk. "You're trying to raise Granny from the dead, little one?" Jane asked. "Ain't nobody laid a hand on her things for at least twenty-five years. Seems it's been a lifetime." She sighed as she blew dust from the top flap of the cardboard box held together by an old string.

"Your Granny was an special old girl," she said as she wrestled with the knot holding the string together. "She'd really be proud of you, little angel," she said, kissing Sally on the forehead. "She'd be claiming that you're a combination of Grandpa and Grandma for sure. Yea! She'd be walking all over the Res right now, bragging about the great things you're gonna be accomplishing."

Jane lifted Sally up on her lap as she finally got the box open. The contents included old letters, pictures and a lot of little things carefully wrapped in different sorts of material. There were also parts of old newspaper clippings, jewellery and an assortment of things Jane couldn't identify. She blew dust off the items. "Never did take the time to check what Granny left in this old trunk," she said to Sally as she carefully lifted a bunch of pictures tied together with red embroidery ribbon. "Maybe you're right, little one, we should have looked through her things years ago."

Jane dusted more pictures off with a cloth. "They collected enough dust sitting here all these years," she said as she carefully separated old yellowed pictures. "People would wonder how well we kept our house if they were to walk in right now."

Sally lost interest in the old things. She started climbing off her mom's lap.

"You be careful around Granny's things now," Jane warned as

Henry Michel

steered Sally away from the trunk. Mom's renewed attention brought Sally's interest to the pictures again. "Dadda, Dadda," she said, pointing to the faded picture. Jane took Sally on her lap. "That's not your Dad, silly girl, that's Grandpa and Uncle Jack," she said. "See, the horses," pointing to the picture "Grandpa and Uncle Jack were always around horses. See that one's Lazy," she said excitedly. "Actually, her real name was Daisy, Grandpa named her that."

"See that old building there?" Sally by now was looking for her bottle. "Nobody would recognize that place today," she continued, "that's where the Mall is now. That building was the old MacKenzie's General Store. It was the biggest store in this valley. People came from all over to shop at that place."

Jane suddenly felt a little embarrassed and checked the room, hoping that no one came in to find her talking in such detail. By now Sally was content with her bottle and soon would be sleeping. Jane carried her to the couch and fixed her a place to lie down. She pulled the rocker over to the shelf near the window by grandma's trunk and sat down.

As she retrieved the pictures, Jane was overcome by a childhood memory. The picture she looked at was another shot of the old MacKenzie store. This time it was a front-view shot. There were wooden chairs and benches in front. It was Stampede time. Grandpa and Grandma sat on one of the large chairs. Grandpa was dressed in his leather vest and a western style shirt while Grandma wore a long plaid dress. Everybody always dressed their best during the stampede. Grandpa's team of horses, along with other teams, was fastened to the side railing of the store, while old cars drove along the street. Where Grandma and Grandpa once sat is where the Mall is now, Jane remembered, and the wooded area by the old store, where she played as a kid, is now all pavement.

Jane remembered the few times she was in town with Grandpa and Grandma; mostly, it was during the summer stampede. She remembered all the Indians camped at the stampede grounds. It seemed that everybody came to the stampede, because she never saw so many people at one time.

One clear memory was the Queen's visit to the Stampede Breakfast at the old Mackenzie Store. Grandpa was always in his glory whenever anybody important came to the stampede breakfast. It was a stampede ritual. Needless to say, everyone in town turned out to hobnob with the Queen. Grandpa was there shaking hands with everybody when the Queen's entourage came by. The Mayor was escorting the Queen. He called out to Grandpa to come over and meet the Queen. Of course, Grandpa had something to say to her. He reminded her that she was in charge of Indians and wanted to know why the Indian Agent didn't bring farm supplies to the reserve any more. He told the Queen, "The Indian Agent said it was too expensive for the government to keep sending farm supplies." Grandpa wanted to know if the Queen had gone broke or if the government had spent all the money that they had taken from Indian land already. "Is that why they couldn't keep paying the Indians?" he asked. Well, Grandpa put that whole Stampede Breakfast in an uproar. Of course, he was just trying to joke with the Queen. He didn't know that he was embarrassing the whole town.

Nobody realizes that that parking lot has so many stories behind it, thought Jane. If the Queen visited there today, would she remember Grandpa or that stampede breakfast? Jane wondered if all the bigwigs in town were still upset with Grandpa for embarrassing them then. How many people still rode their horses to the stampede. And did any of the kids that she grew up with recall the hours they spent playing in that treed lot by the store? "Who remembers how important the old Mackenzie's Store was back then?" she pondered. Now you would never recognize where the store had been.

Just then Sally stirred on the couch. Jane turned her attention to her baby. She questioned the fairness of Sally's life in the city. Nothing here resembled anything she did as a child. How was Sally ever to understand Grandpa, Aunt Annie or any of the people so important to her when she was Jane's age?

The only thing that she had of her childhood was Grandma's things which she kept in the old trunk. She knew Sally needed much more than old memories to appreciate her Grandparents, her little home town, or any of her treasured childhood. Jane had never considered not being part of that life. Now she wondered if she would ever get back to it. She regretted that Sally would never get to know her people if she stayed in the city.

Sally had gotten herself off the couch and demanded attention. Jane carefully placed the things back into the box and into Grandma's trunk. As she walked to the kitchen she became aware of the screech of the rush-hour traffic rattling through the building. Jane realized that she had muted the city noise around her, just as she kept Sally from her family and community. Carrying Sally to the kitchen to get something to eat, she realized that there was nothing in the city for her. Even her apartment seemed foreign. Jane finally understood that Sally should get to know her relatives. She decided she must take Sally home to her own people.

HOME

I

Standing on the side of the highway-
alone on that long stretch of empty road-
she listens for their return

Her body aches in a hundred different places.
A trickle of blood runs down from the cut on her head-
small payment for getting away.

A truck drives up behind her;
the driver offers her a ride.
Through a veil of pain and of fear
she looks at him and tries to figure out if he's safe;
a moment later she gets in.

He's curious; he's concerned.
Wants to take her home to his wife, he says,
"She'll feed you," he promises.

It's been two days since last she ate.
She wants to say yes
but, for the same reason
she would not tell
about being beaten,
she would not say yes
to a meal.
She was afraid to be sent back.
"I'm going home," she tells herself.
"I'm going home; I'm going home.
No more foster homes
because I'm going home;
it's still fifteen hundred miles
but I'm going home."

Arlene Marie Beaumont

                II
A mother opens the door to her two-room suite;
opens it wider when she sees who it is;
doesn't ask a whole lot of questions;
just opens the door to let the girl in.

The young girl stands there
in that dingy little room-
stands there stubbornly
in her exhaustion and pain
"Mom", she says, "I'm not going back"

I'm not going back, her voice says
I'm not going back, her body says
I'm not going back, her spirit says
I'M NOT GOING BACK

The mother looks at her
quietly. She speaks-
with one word
she frees her daughter.
With one word
she welcomes her daughter home

She looks at her daughter
and says
ok.

                III
At another age the woman remembered
herself as that young girl-
Remembered her perilous journey,
her search for a home.

The mother talked about how,
after she spoke to her daughter,
her daughter lay down on her bed
and slept for two days straight.

The daughter slept
in her dirty smelly clothes-
her only possessions-
slept while the cut festered on her head,
slept while her mother looked on.

And the daughter
recognized the strength and respect,
and honoured the wisdom
of the mother's response.

That girl found her home-
with one word
she found her home.

I'm home.

George Anderson

GRANDMA
(Noh Kom)

Grandma was a tiny woman in stature. When you looked down to speak to her, you did not address her as 'Shorty' or any other regrettable thoughts that you had on your mind relating to short people. Perhaps in her early years, if she wore the elevated high heeled shoes of today, she would have reached the height of five feet.

Grandma never let the thought of being short bother her. If she was suspicious that you had in the back of your mind that she was a push-over, forget it; she would soon cut you down to size with her sharp tongue. You see, Grandma was a very outspoken person, much to resembling Charlotte Whitton, the former mayor of the City of Ottawa, who ruled that city like a regimental sergeant-major of a highly disciplined army unit. Charlotte Whitton was a small woman like Grandma. She had the city policemen on their toes at all times. She made it a mandatory ruling that they were always properly dressed and buttoned up despite the hot humid weather and regardless of the temperature measuring one hundred degrees in the shade. Even the taxi drivers adhered to and respected her strict regulation dress; properly dressed with a chauffeur's hat, tie and shirt. You were greeted with courtesy and respect by the chauffeur who opened the door for your entrance to the taxi. Now, one has to struggle with all the parcels or baggage to gain entrance into the taxi. My how times have changed!

If Grandma was not chewing someone's head off she was grumbling at grandpa about the noise we children were making while at play. Luckily, we could not understand her when she was ranting and rumbling on to Grandpa as she was speaking in Saulteaux or Plains-Cree. We children attended a residential school where we were not permitted to speak our native Cree language. Our mother who spoke both dialects always told us children what Grandma was saying. To hear Grandma tell Grandpa her assessment of us children, we were not little angels. But, I suppose we children were not all that bad as not one of us ended up in reform school. In reality, Grandma had her good days. If you were lucky enough to catch her in a good mood, she would even invite you to come over and join her in her small home.

Accepting her invitation, you were careful not to offend her in any way. In her home, you squatted on the floor similar to the Japanese style and custom. If it was meal time and she was in the process of cooking or boiling deer-meat, she would cut off a small portion of the meat in the pot, slice it into fine strips and hand it to you finger style. If you did not relish the idea of her serving it up in this manner, you forced yourself to get it down into your stomach somehow. You did not make it look as though you accidently dropped the meat on the floor as you were already sitting on the floor. If you enjoyed the feast of meat as a delicacy, this made her very happy indeed.

Of course we cannot neglect to mention Ni-chi her faithful guardian dog. Ni-chi was always sitting close to Grandma when it was time to eat. After all he was her prized possession. This was not a high pedigreed dog with a fancy name. He was just an ordinary mongrel dog. I suppose you could probably categorize him as a sooner dog, meaning that he would sooner eat than bite. The only distinguishing aspects of this dog was that he obeyed all his master's instructions in Saulteaux or Cree and he had two golden-yellowish colour spots above his eyes which stood out remarkably well because his hair or coat was a shiny jet black. Faithful to his master this dog was always close at her side.

Ni-chi always sensed or had a premonition when Grandma was about to go out on a stroll. Ni-chi would crouch on the floor on all four legs, nod his head looking at Grandma and let out a bark, as much as to say to his master, "Come on, lets get going." Sometimes he would fool Grandma. At one time or other, dogs have to go to the relief station, whether it be the closest tree or fire hydrant. Ni-chi would go and wait by the door to be let out. Grandma had an abundance of patience with this dog, as she would wait patiently by the door to let him back in. Ni-chi also acted as her seeing-eye dog. Regrettably Grandma's eyesight was not the best. It was a Godsend to have her faithful companion with her at all times.

George Anderson

It has been said, but not proven, that Grandma used to enjoy a little drink of fire-water now and then. It is probably true because on one occasion we dropped in unexpectedly to see Grandma and she was loaded to the ears and singing away in a happy mood; perhaps not in perfect tune, but when a person is fired up like she was who cares. We could not understand how she became so inebriated. You see, the status Indian at that particular time was not allowed to purchase liquor or beer for self-consumption, let alone access to the comforts of sitting in a hotel consuming a beer or two. We later found out that some of our neighbours had picked her up and drove her into town by horse and wagon, which took nearly a day going and returning. Apparently on their arrival in town, they fooled the town-cop by walking into the grocery store, one at a time, and purchasing lemon extract. With small bottles of this size, a person could put a bottle in each pocket and walk out of the store without the town-cop noticing any wrong-doing. So, as you can gather, their way homeward in the horse and wagon resembled a carnival entry in the home-town parade, with lots of singing and laughter and, of course, Ni-chi tagging along behind the wagon.

We children could never understand the strange relationship between our father and Grandma. They never spoke to one another, nor would they make eye contact with each other. If they were to meet head on one would make an about turn and continue to walk on in the opposite direction. It remains a mystery to us. Was this a traditional way of life between mother-in-law and son-in-law? We eventually arrived at the conclusion that Grandma resented our father because our mother married a person who was a non-status Indian. He would never be accepted in the Cree-Saulteaux tribe of people. We also concluded that Grandma, being the outspoken person that she was, gave our father a tongue lashing at an earlier time and he resented it ever since. We thought this was very unlikely because our father was a wounded veteran of two world wars and would probably not put up with treatment by one small woman of stature that would further enhance his war wounds.

IN MEMORY OF MY KOHKUM MADELINE

The oblates of mary immaculate
authorized by the god-he
seized her from a winnipeg orphanage
baptized her "MADELINE"

The department of indian affairs
empowered by an all male government
branded her "INDIAN"
registered her "OSOUP"

My brothers, sisters, and i
brainwashed by
christianity and civilization
saw her only in mooshum's shadow
and we called her "KOHKUM PAUL"

1886
they say she came
to old osoup and his mrs
a malnourished and sickly girl baby
but they loved her fed her
and nourished her life

1894
at eight years old the old blackrobe
uprooted her again reclaimed her for the god-he
imprisoning her youth shaping her mind
fort qu'appelle indian residential school
she simply became #382

there #382's basic education
combined with domestic and industrious training
produced the appropriate INDIAN FARMER'S WIFE
she learned obedience order respect
for god-he, the father, and husband

like a pawn she was traded
between two old men
properly became mrs farmer's wife
she bore him nine children
lived in his shadow for 75 years

in the dim light sometimes i watched
unbraided fiery red hair falling
hanging protective down
the length of her back

i imagined there were plenty
red haired women in ireland
in the dark i thought her eyes
brown sun kissed
they could melt your soul

1979
finally, her life at an end
as she lay dying in that hospital bed
hanging on to each precious moment
waiting for her to mouth
those mysterious irish words

she didn't disappoint me
the last words she spoke
the language of her people
in her last senile moments
MADELINE O'SOUPE ACOOSE #382 whispered
"amo anint wapos, minihkwen nihti"
and motioned for me to sit beside her fire

The Midnight Caller

Elsewhere, but not here
The midnight caller comes
I cannot see him
I know he's there!
My feet throb, continually motion.
A quick glance over the shoulder
eyes glare back.
I hear him behind me,
his breath in gusts!
his heart slamming echoes through my ears.
A quick scan tells me safety's near.
A child's scream echoes across the valley.
I hear an outburst of voices-
feelings of excitement in the air.
I won't let myself slow down!
Driven by fear,
for I know the night stalker is near
A firm grasp on my shoulder.
evil laughter,
shock indulges my body.
Again a child's scream is heard.
A sudden glee, and tears well from my eyes.
A woman takes my hand;
She saves me from the stalker.
She has saved me on previous encounters
She is my mother.
Somehow by a magical incantation the woman,
my mother, removes the evil.
The stalker is gone with a laugh.
My father appears,
sitting in front of the funny box.
He again waits for another night,
He knows the stalker is gone.
What is this place I'm trapped in?

CROSSWORDS

      The little girl would lay
quiet   watching
     the black   and white
boxes in Kye7e's glasses
She'd listen to the squeak squeak of
        Kye7e's pen.

Crosswords and crosswords
Books and books of crosswords.
Kye7e's words, hundreds and hundreds of words,
        Across and Down words
French and Latin
Spanish and German,
Regular words and abbreviated words.
Past tense words,
Words across the whole puzzle
and two letter words meaning a SW direction.

Reflections in Kye7e's glasses.
Reflections of realms and realms of knowledge
        Hidden
        Except in those
        Books and books of finished

        Crosswords, dusty
        Under the bed.

Leona Hammerton

Longtime Ago-and Now
[for Andy]

I have taken your hand
as we walked
through an abandoned
one-room shack
My home once

Tiny shoes and Sally Anne rubber boots
litter the floor
A sardine tin soapdish
droops from a rusty nail
Where there used to be a kid-height
wash basin stand

Our eyes open to rubble and my mind
screams that this is not the way it was
a broken table - legs missing -
once held a beautiful bouquet
of mismatched silver in a
Roger's Syrup tin vase
One room of memories
I forgot to tell you things

Brothers' and sisters' laughter
still echo in my ears
And my Mom sewed her heart
into the arms and legs of a rag doll
bigger than me
My Mom sewed her heart into button eyes
and red thread smile
and rag-doll-clothes

I can laugh
when I remember packing water
and swinging the bucket
around and around, just right,
without spilling one drop

Leona Hammerton

And I can cry
when I know
that fresh-brewed coffee smell
and hot deer stew and bannock
won't fill that room again

You have taken my hand
as we walked
through an abandoned shack
and we sat quietly under pine trees
where a swing once brought
belly-laughs
and high pitched screams of delight
And the contrast
of our worlds merged
and fit more snugly -
merged
and held us safe -
And when I closed my eyes
I saw a beautiful
Rag-Doll-nod
and the broadest
red-thread smile

The Green Chief

My wife comes home from work exhausted, throws off her coat, collapses into our old plump easychair and tells me that something has to be done about the traffic. Even though she refuses to drive during rush hour, preferring instead to take the bus, the jam, the noise and stink of it all makes her feel as though she's the one in the driver's seat. Thank goodness she's not is all I can say, both for her and the car, not to mention everybody else on the road. (Imagining her voice a sheet of stilled panic, knuckles white, clutched to the steering wheel, eyes full of twisted expectation as the vehicle lunges to a halt.)

"Didn't someone say that we live in the age of anxiety," I ask as I massage her shoulders, knuckles digging into muscle.

"Age of ignorance," she answers, while she oohs and aahs.

"I wonder if they'll ever invent something to replace them - the cars and trucks, I mean?"

"Not as long as the oil companies have anything to say about it," she concludes matter-of-factly.

"Maybe a few more giant oil spills like the Exxon Valdez, or that one off California, and the public will finally say enough is enough."

"Since when has Mr. & Mrs. Citizen had any say?" she grumbles, the black heat of the street still inside her.

"I was listening to a program the other day on C.B.C. about some Scot who, something like twenty-five years ago, moved to Newfoundland because it was one of the few places where they still used horses... guess he liked horses. The pace, probably."

"Sounds like a smart man," she says and indicates, with her right hand clasped to her left shoulder, that I should massage closer to the left side of her spine. Obliging, my knuckle probes deep, releasing a gasp of relief.

"But they're almost all gone now," I feel compelled to add, realizing too late that such a small comment can shatter so much.

"A shame," she says, then, after a moment of silence, "think of it, horses clomping down the road, sleigh rides in the winter."

"The fragrance of horse shit," I quietly add, again digging my fingers into the shoulder muscle. "Loosen up."

"Ouch! Easy." She twists. "There's nothing better for roses than horse manure. Where I come from a few of the farmers still use horses. My mother makes sure she carries a plastic bag with her when she goes to the market so she can pick some up for her garden."

She's got a point. I've seen her mother's flowerbeds, and I admit they're quite spectacular: gladioli, lilies, geraniums, roses - among others which I don't know the names of. All smelling sweet and shitty.

"So how was your day?" she asks, standing and rolling her shoulders.

"I'm working on a story, I'm not sure where it's heading but it's got to do with Chief Seattle."

"You sure it's even a story?" she laughs, "Last time all those notes you took ended up being a four line poem, or was it three?"

I'm not sure how to take this last comment, but she's right. Even in this age of the computer, which might also be termed the age of input diarrhoea, fingers punch away at keyboards like there's no tomorrow, I find myself with the spectacular ability to edit myself into silent oblivion. Like the Invisible Man in that old movie, my words are the bandages which I unwrap, or more particularly either strike or scratch out, until there's nothing left of me. The invisible silent ghost man floating around the room. Instead of a pair of dark sunglasses, all you see is a pen or pencil riding on my invisible ear.

"Chief Seattle? Why him? You're not from the west coast. And besides, remember all that fuss at Enviro-House?"

"Fuss...Don't exaggerate."

"Ohh, that feels good. Thanks, honey," is all she says, unwilling to dwell on the unpleasant, now that she has shed her twist of highway; instead she arches her back - stretches and then pecks me on the cheek.

About a month ago we were downtown and happened to walk into one of those environmental stores that seem to be popping up like mushrooms all over the country. Frankly, she was the one who first noticed the multicoloured pile of tee-shirts and brought them to my attention, as I busied myself leafing through some expensive magazine which had a feature article on composting. Something I never really thought you had to read about, but which happened rather naturally. As for the tee-shirts, I think she was thinking of buying one for my birthday. I could tell by the gleam in her eye. And so I thought it best that I head her off at the pass, to use a rather quaint expression.

"Look," she said. "Aren't these pretty?"

"Perfect," I answered flatly, checking out the design, an American eagle swooping off into a sunset above the portrait of a wise stern face. Chief Seattle with his words of wisdom below the picture. It was all there. They hadn't missed a note, except maybe the flaming arrows. Everything we always needed to get ourselves in touch with Mother Earth but were afraid to wear until now, I think I was thinking at the time but didn't say. Or did I?

Needless to say, I never did get that tee-shirt for my birthday and, in fact, never gave a further thought to the old Chief. As for the little "fuss" (to quote my wife) in the store amid the herbal soaps and sponges, tonics and shampoos, rainforest crunch and carob bars, what happened was that I ended up buying the tee-shirt for my wife and trying my best to forget all about it. To put it plainly, it wasn't until I came across a column in yesterday's paper that I dredged up the scene and got to thinking about Chief Seattle again, about what he might or might not have actually said. You see, according to the article, all those things accredited to him he never did actually say.

In other words, the myriad of messages on all those tee-shirts and wall posters are supposedly made-up, fabricated, invented, all that profundity... that... wisdom, such as the "Earth does not belong to man; man belongs to the Earth. What is man without beasts? If all the beasts were gone, men would die from a great loneliness of spirit. For whatever happens to the beasts, soon happens to man. The whiteman treats his mother, the Earth, and his brother, the Sky, as things to be bought, plundered and sold like sheep or bright beads. His appetite will devour the Earth and leave behind only a desert." All those famous and I might add, marketable, quotable quotes concocted by some environmentalist who realized that the message wouldn't fly under his own name; what was needed was (and again I quote) "sentimentalized Indian environmentalism."

This, then, is what I'm relating to my wife, who is now asking me to unzip the back of her skirt so that she can slip into something more comfortable - like jeans and a tee-shirt. I tell her that I find the allegations simply fascinating, my reaction one of scorn and amusement.

"What a scam," I say. "What a ploy, but how can anybody know for sure, unless maybe the ghost writer himself confessed. And then, how do we know he's not just trying to grab the limelight?"

To appropriate or not to appropriate, the question of the day itself usurped, which now becomes to fabricate or not to fabricate. Or better yet, to fib or not to fib.

I can see from her furrowed eyebrows that she is taking in all that I'm saying, mulling over it, composting it – if you like – stirring it up, laying the freshness out in her mind.

"Context," she finally says, wiggling out of her skirt, right here in the living room.

"What?"

"Did the article you read mention what was happening in the mid-nineteenth century and even earlier? Repercussions? Legacy?"

"No, why would it?"

"Think about it," she answers, moving to the sofa and peeling off her stockings.

So I do, think, I mean, while I sit back for a moment and watch her and then, so as not to get side tracked, I go over to the bookcase and pull out reference books.

One thing for sure, by 1855 (the time of Chief Seattle's supposed speech) the writing was on the wall or, as we might now say, on the billboards.

Highlights: In 1851, London, Queen Victoria opened the Great Exhibition of the Works of Industry of All Nations, now commonly referred to as the first Worlds Fair.

The Industrial Revolution, already begun in the last century with the introduction of the spinning jenny and the steam engine, was booming and expanding business so that unfettered growth had now become a means to an end.

Addressing the cost of the Industrial Age in human terms, Charles Dickens, in England, wrote Bleak House in 1853 and Hard Times in 1854.

By 1867, Canada's ambition to settle the west was national policy.

In 1790, the United States was comprised of 892,000 square miles, and by 1910, 3,754,000 and still consuming.

What was to prevent such an expansion? Nothing. Absolutely. Or, as the book I am consulting bluntly states — written in 1955, exactly 100 years after Chief Seattle's famous or now infamous speech — "Save for a few Indians of Stone Age culture the land in the late eighteenth century was almost empty."

"There you have it," she says, getting up to go and get her clothes.

"What?"

"That the end justifies the means... always has."

"You mean primitive in one era, wise and witty in another?"

"You got it."

And in a Doris Day singsong voice, I burst out, "Que Sera,

Sera... Whatever we'll be we'll be."

"Something like that," she says, leaving the room.

Quotation upon quotation. Truth in Lie. Lie in Truth. And in her trail of late afternoon shadow, my mind flips to another tidbit of information, that during the industrial expansion some of the rivers in those American industrial towns were so dirty that they actually caught fire. All the while the elite, Carnegie, Rockefeller, Edison, Ford... were wining and dining, celebrating their idea of civilization and success.

And I picture a dark oak room, crystal lit, grey men in tails, with drink in hand, gazing contently at the rings of blue smoke they blow from their cigars. Their faces smug and full, their eyes blank, they don't understand what they're looking at, what they're doing.

Then the book I've been reading falls to the floor, and I turn towards the windows, the falling day rising red.

And in the lingering moment of light, Chief Seattle, riding a crest of fire, a river gone mad, stands before me, beckoning me to travel and yet stay where I am, because it is here, here, inside, below the fire, in the calm, the blue, the green, where the connection lies. In beauty. He tells me in perfect silence, "You have heard it before, it is not new, it is as old as we are, they are, all of us. It is survival and beyond."

And I look into his face. It's so bright, sunlight through afternoon rain; it's every face I've ever seen that speaks with words of water that wash over body, mind and spirit, cleanse and free. Fluid, drinkable, timeless.

And with a flourish of his arms he opens wide the blanket of sky that he has, until this moment, kept wrapped tightly round him. And there, inside, is the Earth, mother of us all, spinning blue and green in a cushion of cloud set among stars.

It is at that moment that she enters the room, fresh from changing her clothes, fresh in her womanhood, Chief Seattle now a picture on her tee-shirt blazing a path across her breast, his words a pattern of the present, a flight to here and now. And she with her smile ready to go out into the garden.

salvaged

i. breathing words

my whispers flee to you through tree tops
as though you will remember
a sound between breaths
then there's you
standing firm
solid as the mountain people of your ancestry
softly speaking words of your making
to women and men who cannot
keep secrets
all while my voice
slides to the ground
(you are forgiven of course)
and the wind grows silent as a shadow
(or so i imagine)

ii. skywriting

pale are the lines of my thought
against the sky blueness
of your presence

iii. talking sticks and breaking bones

sometimes i cannot speak without
flinching: the distances between planets disappear
so that we fall together
crushed by mutual attraction
of this am i afraid
"your turn!" you say winking
so i can only laugh and forget to look down
seeing you now i predict
later in your life you will turn to the moon
finding solace in her face

k. damm

iv. just thinking

maybe it's just that i can see
the light traces of lines
that i know will grow into deep furrows
etched earnestly into our skin
maybe it's just the way the dry leaves swirl
like scraps of parchment
long unread
maybe it's just how the babies have learned to speak
and run and dream
since last we spoke in the hushed tones
of two sharing secrets
maybe it is all that and more
that leaves me yearning
for your voice and the soft fingers
of newly-formed words

OCHRE LINES

skins
drums
liquid beat fluttering under the breast
coursing long journeys
through blue
lifelines
joining body to body
primeval maps
drawn under
the
hide
deep
floating dreams past
history
surging forward
upward
through indigo passages
to move on the earth
to filigree into fantastic
gropings over the land
journeys marking
red trails
a slow
moving earth vision

Heart Butte dance

a fall wind arrived whirling and drying out
summer dreams and travelling clothes.
scented with promises of wood smoke, and edged with ice
it swept us together.
> idle chatter surrounded our hearts,
> fluid and warm words passed over our
> tongues and minds.

the sounding of brass dance bells
stalled the evening's end.
> a breeze passed beneath my heavy dress,
> brushing my uncovered thighs.

duties and diversions pressed against our bodies.
parting with no touches,
> true desires silenced by the past.

whispers of winter time dreams blew against my back.

Nine month blues

Mouthwatering moans escape your lips
smirking
you dare to dream without me!

Comfortably settled beside me
amongst my nest
of piled pillows and tangled blankets
your snore is like
fingernails grating over chalkboard
selfish
you dare to sleep before me!

Wrestling the night
determined to master a position of relief
my yearning body
swells
confined in transition
fingers numb
starve for circulation
deep sighs erupt
I remain saturated with frustration
while I watch you
unconscious
you lay oblivious to my needs.

Paralysed pride
hides my naked vulnerability
I lay dormant beside your
unfamiliar depressions
choking in my freedom
my silent scream
wavers above your ears
to remind you
I am Gypsywoman!

Kelly Terbasket

I have no need
for your breath
to tingle warm words of assurance
across my neck.

I have no need
for your satiny fingers
to stroke my straining body.

I have no need
for your gaze to rest gently
in admiration of my motherhood.

It's A Baby

After much pain
It was late
and then it was early

I don't know how long it took
I was there
lying then squatting and then
I paced along corridors long
and lean
I held onto railings along the way
Bending myself to stop the pain

No It hurts
No, no, no
Stop the pain

I carried on and took some time
I managed

White ladies touched me
trying to silence my voice
they checked me
dilation

progress

still it stayed
for quite some time
small
It won't be long they told me
they told him
help me breathe
My Mother held me close
I bit her shoulder to
stop my pain

Gunargie O'Sullivan

Ouch she moaned
brushing the pain away
Ouch

The lights were bright
I closed my eyes
I called out loud
I controlled my voice
so carefully
steady sounds escaped my lips
So precious chants of the days so old
They help me make it through

Overnight it happens
overnight
Not what I expected
I push real hard
I breathe steadily
I used my voice as old as I can

Stop that they say
Don't use your voice
use your breathing

exercise

your voice
too loud
patience
wonder what is going on?

stop the shrills stop the sounds

No I said no
It's helping me
I don't care what the people think
I don't care what anyone says
I continue using my voice
to control

Gunargie O'Sullivan

my own way

I'm moved
My time is near
A birthing room is where I am
I close my eyes to see shadows of bright light
I am hot and I am cold

How long will this take
I squirm and I salivate
I try to let gravity take weight

Now push
don't waste another one
push

I sleep
I wake
I look
They look at me
Four women
One man

My man looks to me
I search for his question

What will they all do
Help me I Plead
Help
They just stand

I wonder what for
Do something

Why are they even here
I close my eyes and contemplate

I reach for the skies in my mind
One hand up the other clenched to covers

Gunargie O'Sullivan

Birthing bed
I breathe out my breath
While I wait for another

I am told to push harder
I am told try harder
I am told
help the baby
I am told
I try

Come on baby my mum and man say
Come on baby you can do it
We know you can
remember when we used to say what you can do
you can do anything
You can do anything you set your mind to
Shut up I say
as I suck on ice

Shut up

fuck it hurts
I focus on the sky

I give up
I can't do this any more

come on now
Fuck
come on now

Breathe
Push
And breathe

Last push
as hard as I can
I push

One more
And another
One more time
And another
And another and another
I can

Oush

There comes the baby

She's here baby I hear
he and she say
She's here baby
The baby's here
Look
look
It's our baby girl
It's our baby
I look but I am too tired to see

Donna K. Goodleaf

Mother

I dedicate this poem to my mother and all the mothers and Grandmothers and Women of all the Red Nations of Turtle Island

mother,
there you were sitting at the head of the table
like always, a place that is sacred to your daughters and sons
smoking and sipping on coffee talking and laughing with father
and my brothers in the early hours of the morning when the sun
begins to rise

my eyes look to my brothers
dressed in fatigues, ready to protect and defend our people, our land,
ready to sacrifice their lives for our children
they take one last drag and one last sip of coffee with you and
father before they go on barricade duties

as I stood by the fridge, tears filled my eyes
I looked at you and saw the heaviness of pain etched around your eyes
I felt your heart pounding to the rhythm of fear
the heaviness of fear, the fear of losing your sons
the fear and pain of not knowing whether this would be the last
morning of greeting your sons with love
would this morning ritual be broken?

as my brothers got up and puffed on their last cigarette
their eyes looked to you for comfort
your beauty of love and strength flew like a whirlwind into their hearts
your beauty of love and strength eased their fears of this war
your beauty of love and strength had protected and carried them
back home safely each night

Nia'wen:kowa mother, for bringing my brothers home safely each night

My Little Child

The water is flowing
Ever so gentle, you
can hear it.
She sits in a field.
Flowers, butterflies,
Kissing the petals,
The sun shines on,
The rocks, the rocks,
Giving strength, energy,
She sits,
She is of the sun, the flowers
The rock, the water,
She lives.
My little child,
She turns,
She smiles,
I wave.

PRE-PARENTHOOD

It was noon or maybe just after. I had just finished cooking lunch and doing the dishes. I sat in the living room and put my feet up on the coffee table. Jacqueline made her way up the stairs as a typical pregnant woman would. She had one hand on the back of her hip, and the other supported our future in her belly. It felt good to rest my feet, I thought. I thought too soon.

"Russ!" she called, without seeing me on the couch. "Can we go to the store? I've got this craving for Yogurt-Oh!" she said, surprised. "I thought you were in the kitchen washing the floor. I thought you said you were going to wash the floor?" she said sarcastically.

I grumbled to myself and started for the kitchen.

"Can we go to the store?" she asked again.

"Well, what's it going to be, the kitchen or the store?" I forced the issue, although knowing all the while that I was masterfully escaping the dreaded housework.

"Well," she added, "I could take the truck."

Oh! oh! I thought.

"No, it's okay," I said cleverly. "I know how much you hate to drive. Maybe I'd better go with you just to make sure there isn't an accident. I wouldn't want anything to happen to you or baby coo."

That's what she called her.

Jacqueline smiled and shook her head.

"Let's go. Baby coo's hungry."

We headed down the road to I.G.A. to pick up some milk, bread, and other necessities, like ice-cream, yogurt, pickles, and bananas. On the way there, we saw a man and a woman walking down the road. They were clearly upset. The man pointed across the street, and his wife ran over to the other side. She was definitely looking for something. The look on the man's face got me thinking. He mouthed something to his wife and pointed ahead of himself toward the creek that runs down along the side of the road. I kept driving, but I watched in the rear view mirror. I contemplated going back to offer my assistance. I had a feeling that something was drastically wrong. I convinced myself that it was a pre-paternal instinct, and I had to do something about it. I wouldn't be able to live with myself if something terrible happened and I didn't help when I had the chance. I mentioned to Jackie that maybe they had lost their child.

Soon all we could think about was a poor little child lost. I thought to myself, maybe someone had abducted their little girl. It had to be a her, because the doctor told us that our baby was going to be a little girl. So, naturally, every time I think about children, my mind kicks in. "Beep! beep! beep! Little girl! Little girl!" Anyway, my thoughts jumped to the river. I pictured a little girl floating face down. Her pigtails were slightly under water weighted down by tiny little pink barrettes.

That's it! I thought, I'm going back to help that couple find their little child! I told Jackie how I felt, and I didn't have to twist her arm. It was already wrapped around and rubbing her tummy. Her worried straining face told me it was the right thing to do. I waited for a stretch of road. When I could see it was clear, I did a U-turn as fast as I could. On the way back I noticed that the creek was frozen over. I started to feel embarrassed.

"Well, she never fell in the creek," I said to Jackie, pointing to the ice. "She might've fell through the ice somewhere," Jackie returned nervously. Oh, Great! I thought with a sigh. We drove beside the man as he walked quickly down the roadside. His head turned toward the truck. The look on his face assured me once again that something terrible had happened. I would rather have been embarrassed and mistaken. I felt so sorry for this poor couple. I couldn't imagine losing our baby. Gee! What if they thought we took their baby? Don't be silly, I thought, don't jump to conclusions. I took a deep breath and zipped down the power window on Jackie's side. I thought to myself that I better hurry and say my piece. I didn't want the fella to think I might have good news and then disappoint him by telling him that I was only offering to help. I took a deep breath and said to him uneasily.

"Hi there I noticed that you and your wife looked quite distressed, and I wanted to know if you needed any help?" I guess I spoke fast enough, because the look on his face never changed. Although he didn't want to give out any information, I could tell. He tried not to make it look as bad as I knew it was. Oh! It was bad! I could see it in his eyes. My heart went out to him. This was the most tragic thing I'd ever been a part of.

"No, that's okay. We're just looking." He paused for a second. I knew he was swallowing his pride. Sometimes, parents don't like to admit their mistakes, but he seemed to be about to. Maybe, if I press just a little bit further.

"You sure? Four sets of eyes would be better than two." I shivered to myself. Lost child, what a shame. He shouldn't feel bad, though. A person can't take full responsibility for the way the world is today. I felt sick to my stomach. I pictured some rubby-dub-looking character with long oily hair hanging down on his tattered jean jacket. I imagined him with a three-day-old beard. It partially hid a scar that he would have got while in prison. He was carrying a young girl of about four years of age. She was kicking, screaming and crying as he forced her into a beat-up old Ford. It would have to be a Ford. Nobody driving a G.M. would ever do something so terrible, I hoped. Oh my God! We have to find this poor innocent child before she's taken away. She may be sold on some kind of black market and forced into slavery in a foreign country. That would be terrible.

"You sure everything is all right?" I kept pressing.

"Yeah, thanks any way, we're just looking... for... our..." Everything seemed to slow down. Oh! No! he's looking for his dog, not his daughter. I started to feel my face turning red. I pictured a tiny sandy brown dog with long hair. Its hair was longer than its short little legs. It had a yellow ribbon dangling from its hair. It was wandering down by the creek, whining, like little dogs do when they want something or when they're lost. Its fur was getting dusty from being on its own for so long. A ribbon hung loosely where it once was tied firm. It was ready to collapse on the ground. That would make it difficult for us to tell whose dog it was. If their dog had a ribbon in its hair and the one we found didn't, how were we supposed to know if it was theirs or not. Nope! it had to be a child, and I had to force the issue.

"Let me help you sir," I said abruptly. "I know you're trying to be strong but..." I paused for a second.

"What are you talking about?" he said with a look of confusion on his face.

"It's okay," I cut in "I understand. I realize your position. I wouldn't want anyone to know that I let my daughter get stolen from me either!"

"What!" he yelled "Something's happened to my little Lorrie?" Oh! that's her name I said to myself. What a shame!

"Marg!" the guy screamed frantically. His wife came running

around a corner within seconds.

"My God, Marg, something's happened to Lorrie!"

"What is it! What is it!" she screamed.

By this time, Jackie was elbowing me in the ribs.

"Russ! Russ! I think..."

Shhh! I cut her off.

"Lorrie's been abducted," the man said, anxiously comforting his wife with his arms. As soon as he told her, she broke into tears.

"No, not my baby!" she cried. "She was just ahead of me only a few moments ago." It was horrible. My worst thoughts were coming true. Their poor little baby girl had been taken from them. My god, we have to find her.

"Russ! Russell!" Jackie insisted.

"What the heck do you want?" I said in frustration.

"I don't think that they..." she was cut off by a young teenage girl's voice.

"Hey Mom, Dad, I found the top for the stove. It must have blown out of the truck. Some guy was carrying it up the road, over there." She pointed down the street.

"What!" I said, in disbelief.

"Oh! No! I'm sorry. I thought that..." The people never heard me; they just rushed to their daughter and hugged her. I turned red, dropped the truck in gear and stepped on the gas. Jackie laughed all the way down each of the back alleys to the I.G.A.

"Hope we never see them again," I said, embarrassed.

Anna Kruger

MY SON SHINE
To my son Elliott

It was a beautiful sunny day
when you entered the world
weighing in at 8lbs. 3oz.
my son, Shine

I almost lost you twice
while I was carrying
you inside me
I fought not to lose my baby
I wanted a girl so bad

I cried when the doctor said
You have a beautiful baby boy
No I wanted a girl
I already had my son
the apple of my eye
my firstborn, my son

I cried those bitter tears of disappointment
until the nurse placed
your perfect little body in my arms
my son, Shine

I looked into your beautiful blue eyes
I knew at that moment that I could not
love you any less than my firstborn
you were my son, Shine

Anna Kruger

I have never regretted your being
from that moment on
To this very day
I can still feel
the warm sensation in my heart
every time I look into your eyes
or when I see your smile
my son, Shine

You are my son, Shine
You make me happy
when the skies are gray
Please don't take
my son Shine away

Grandma Marie Potts

      She was grandma to everyone,
even us older people.
When she came to
the Bear Dance, we would
all crowd around her car
to welcome her.
      She'd cock her head
at an oldtimer
and say something in Maidu
and they'd have
a fast back and forth
then both
burst into laughter.
      She'd only rest
a short time in the house
then begin
asking questions
which were
directions for setting
the camp in order.
      Children gathering
firewood and carrying
water, women
and girls
already cooking,
the men
starting to butcher
and lighting the fire
in the roasting pit.
      Tents
would be going up
for two days,
children
all over the place.

Peter Blue Cloud/Aroniawenrate

    At sunrise ceremony
she stood
dressed in doeskin
holding
a bright flicker band.

    And that's how I see her
now.
    And when
she passed away,
we all of us hurt
for a long time.
    And I wonder
if others saw
what I did:
    her great-grandchildren
dancing,
    grandma's eyes
looking from them.

Nga Roimata

Girl of sorrow, tears spell your name
Your cry burst out as the green leaves
Welcomed this mourner, this
time traveller, this
manuhiri arriving in dread
In the fading light
Broken, I came

The breath of the Dark Lady swirled in the uncarved
    house
I heard her sighing in the welcoming speeches
I felt her sobbing in the ritual embrace
I came out of respect for her
To stand between her and you -
Pale in your black clothes
Watching beside your small white-boxed treasure
Pink camellia clusters laid out above
Your unlined face too young for this
This is unseasonal
That coffin should be full sized, man sized, the body
    in it old

Next day the busload that had travelled all night
One high-pitched tangi outside the house pierced the
    morning
Black-clad women wailing, green fronds threading
    their hair
Even a moko blue on the chin
Advancing in response to the shrill karanga
Family photos carried in front, hands green waving
You sat there taking the grieving, you waited
Your face impassive, your crying done for a time
Your breasts were bursting, they had to be bound
Your child could not suck at that food, nor pull at
    your pendant to get it

Rain misty between the house and the kitchen
Ringawera worked through the night
The new block dining hall there in front, almost
    completed
The heaped builder's mix an improvised sandpit
In the meantime we slithered in mud so the wait
    could go on
Speeches and singing, argument and prayer
The small fat face colder and greyer

After three days we emerged into clear air
The sea limpid blue currents below
The islands, green and brown, sharp silhouetted in
    their pattern
We walked again down that winding clay road
To where clay deeper dug would clasp
the tiny body to the breast of Papatuanuku
assisted by leather-coated spadesmen
Handfuls of earth crumbled between the fingers,
    flowers

In the small church, murmured incantations,
and the host of kohanga reo children
sat on the floor up front
They were an observant congregation
They were witnesses
This was children's business

The low lamentation of waves greeting the shore
echoed our weeping, girl
Let your tears of grief cover the sky
Your ancestor, double arched Uenuku
will give you his sign to stand
Battle on,
Find the sun again

Sheilia Austin

TIME TO LET GO...

Please Great-grandmothers and Great-grandfathers
of our ancestors
Come forward and show our loved ones the way
Help them to pass over to the spirit world.

We have faith in the Creator
To guide our loved ones
From sunrise to sunset.

It is time for us to let go
To allow them to pass into the spirit world
Where there is no pain or discomfort.
There is only contentment
Contentment with our ancestors.

We must remember to free ourselves
To travel our individual paths here on earth
From sunrise to sunset
Until our time comes to join our Creator
In the spirit world.

We will always carry our loved ones
In our hearts and minds.
But, we must release them
From our earthly pulls
To allow them to pass over to the spirit world
To the next step in their journey.

HONOR SONG FOR MOTHERS OF COURAGE

Good Spirits bless the child
    born of a mother
A little mother
    so young herself
Who alone must decide
    whether to end a life
before it has been birthed
Alone
    alone
        alone
With mother's love
    to decide
A life to give
    to a little helpless one.

Sacred circles form in
    mother's eyes
Around
    such a child
So fortunate
    finding life instead of
    silence
Finding
    a welcome path from
    dark warm womb
To see the sun
    and mother's smile.

Nature's mothers fight
    with tooth and claw
    to shield their little ones
Giving up life itself
    sacrificing all
That they might live.

Jack D. Forbes

The Great Holy Mystery
    with eagle feathers
    touches the hair of
Mothers who
    through tears and pain
    overcoming fear and suffering
Courageously
    unselfishly
Give the gift of life to the
    little one inside.

Hard enough
    to give birth
Harder still
    to face the world
Alone
    with a child to feed
"I have my career"
    some might say
"How can I ever find a man"
    others might think
"What a curse, what bad luck
    brings this child"
    despairing voices mock.

But looking inside
    our little mother
Sees the child within
    and using love as her prayer
Reaches out to
    holy messengers
Carrying her
    songs of motherhood
Sacred hoops of melody
    around the wholeness
    of this Our Mother Earth
    who never deserts
    her children.

Songs of mothers are always holy
    always pure
But songs of
    courageous mothers
    single mothers
Have special power
    reaching the little heart
    beating below
    and giving strength
    to a
Chosen child.

Some little mothers must
    as fate decrees
Give up their child
    to be adopted
As a chosen one to brighten the life
Of one who cannot have a child
    such an act
    cannot be judged
    or condemned
For the decision may come
    from the love within
And be the mother's way of
    fighting for her
    little one
A terrible sacrifice
    to be made.

The mother who chooses to raise
    her child
Must also many sacrifices make
    but she is
    gifted in return
By a child's love for her.

I was chosen by a mother, although differently,
    one who risked her life
    for me

Jack D. Forbes

My birth was very hard for her
    and maybe
    that is why
I say prayers of
    thanks
And love all my mothers
    in this way.

Little Mothers of this earth
    I sing a song
    an honor song
To celebrate you
    for all to hear
For the world to know
    I hold you dear
And not me alone
For I know
    the Spirits sing
    honor songs
And form
    sacred circles
    around you
With their feet
    as they dance
    heads bowed
With profound respect.

Mothers of courage
Mothers of strength
    the gift of pride
You have won
    counting coup
Against most dangerous foes
    in hard battle
With coup sticks brightly feathered
    and painted
With bands of love and
    selflessness.

Mothers of courage
Mothers of strength
    the gift of pride
You win every day
    struggling to make ends meet
    facing the winds of
Whispered jealousy and foul-mouthed
    hypocrisy
Facing storms of prejudice and
    poverty
Loneliness, perhaps at times,
    and tears.

Mothers
    little mothers
Of courage
    of strength
I say a prayer
    smoke a sacred pipe
For you
    and my smoke rises
    encompassing in its cloud
    all motherhood.

Mothers of men
    mothers of women
        mothers of this Our Mother Earth
I give thanks to you
    source of my own life.

    Wanishi!

And to the Great Spirit,
    Grandfather,
In humbleness
    I a poor boy
Pray
    asking
    from my deepest being

Jack D. Forbes

have pity on these Our Mothers
    Grandfather
Have pity on them
    and shield them from the winds
Adding to their strength
    giving them the knowledge
    of your love
    your sacred medicine.

With my legs running I form a
    sacred circle
Around these Our Mothers of Courage
Hear my prayer
    Grandfather
Wanishi!
    Bless All My Relatives.

REBIRTH

fearing, fearing
    leaving, leaving
        sliding, sliding
            growing, growing

Fearing the unknown. Leaving the old behind and reaching for new, yet old horizons. Sliding into new experiences. Growing beyond places ever hoped for or dreamed of. Blue skies, white fluffy clouds. Beautiful sunsets. Roaring oceans. Lapping, comforting sounds of the precious waters. Majestic mountains speaking. My family, my own people, other Nations. Beautiful people. Young men with old souls. Old women with young spirits. Young women with a never ending drive for life. Babies, with clear sparkling eyes. New and precious life.

pushing, pushing
    screaming, screaming
        embracing, embracing
            pushing, pushing

Push, push. Don't hold yourself back. Don't let the pull of the old, pull you down. Cry. Don't cry. Scream, let yourself scream. Scream to hear your silenced voice. Scream to release the old pain. Embrace life. Spirit taking me by the hand. Don't be afraid. Don't hold yourself back. The unknown darkness is you. The unknown darkness is our ancestors guiding you. Giving you strength. Embrace it all — look, see, touch, feel, smell. Allow yourself new life, it is yours. Push, push. Keep pushing onto the new and familiar shores. Explore the new horizons of yourself to reach your inner peace.

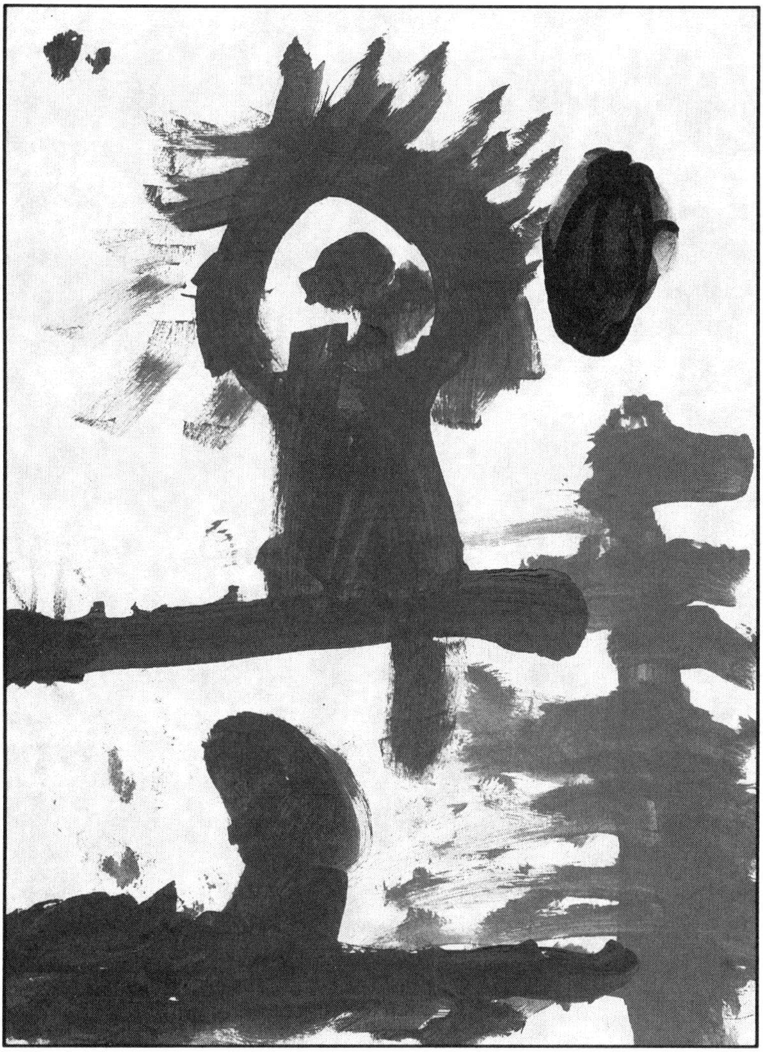

Children

Deanna Kimball

Original Woman

Our weakness is our minds.
Our strength is our hearts
Or is it reversed?
Original wo/man had an original mind.
Every action had soul, depth
Like the falling sun in the sky of the West

Original wo/man lived in silent peace
She/he roamed the land with a strong mind, heart,
Now our weakness is our minds, heart.
Acknowledging the bad spirits
Just to ensure a healthy life and way.
That's how she/he lived.
She/he lived under the sky and above the earth.
She/he lived with the animals and for each other.
She/he prayed to Gilwedin, to White Buffalo.
She/he prayed to Waaban, to Golden Eagle.
She/he prayed to Zhaawan, to Mouse.
She/he prayed Ningaabi, to Black Bear.
Original wo/man had not only a great mind but
great heart.

She/he prayed to Mama'aki.
She/he prayed to Papa'giizi.
She/he prayed to Nookomis.
She/he prayed to Nimishomis.
Where is our spirit, our strength?
Who among us prays to the four directions.
    to our Mother Earth
    to our Father Sun
    to our Grandmother Moon
    to our Grandfather Rock?

Where are you Original wo/man?

The Medallion

The year was 1850.

The sky was blue with a shade of purple.
The trees were nothing but a dark shadow looking at you. Stars twinkled. Old Man's beard moss hung off of every tree limb. The trail was so quiet. "BANG!" A gun went off. You could hear the echo for a mile. About fifty long haired Indians swarmed to the south side of the trail. An American popped out. He had a clear shot at the nearest Indian, only fifty feet away. There was a bright shine glinted the Indians medallion as he fell to the ground. "BANG"!!! (The echo slowly died out)

(Dr. Dre's music playing in the background)

"Waz up!" says Joe to Trevor. "Waz up!" Trevor replied.
"You got to jet if you don't want to be late for work," said Joe. "Yeah call me later." said Trevor.

Trevor was an Indian who worked at a local gas station about a mile from where he lives. He is staying at his friend Joe's. Trevor had run away from his parents house when they were fighting. Trevor was already late for work. He thought he would take a short cut through the war trail, even though he had never gone that way before. Trevor had been walking for about twenty minutes into the trail, when he began to think that if anything happened, no one would hear. As he got deeper and deeper into the forest it got darker. Trevor stopped and looked behind himself. Nothing. Slowly he turned around and heard, "La la la la la la." It was so loud that his ears started ringing.

"BANG!" He heard the last gun shot of the 1850 war. It slowly echoed through the forest to slowly die away. Trevor kneeled down on the ground holding his ears. He was very shaky. He didn't know what to expect next. He turned around quickly to see a medallion hanging off a branch. The tree was so ugly and twisted he was scared to touch it. As he picked up the shiny disk he completely forgot about being late for work. This strange medallion was made of four substances: wood, gold, bronze, and silver. Each material accounted for one quarter of the complete circle.

Tommy Paul

On the back of the medallion were the words "ONE DAY YOU WILL BE FREE OF WHAT IS KILLING US ALL." Trevor did not know what this meant. He said to himself, "This is crazy. I'll just go sell it for some beer this weekend." He began to head for work again. But when he looked ahead, a man stood before him. The man had a scar going down the outside of the left leg. He had long black hair in two braids. He had a strong build. He too was an Indian. The man said with a deep voice. "YOU ARE LEAVING, DYING, AND NOT FREE." Trevor said "Free of what? Who are you? What do you want with me? I didn't do anything."

The man replied "Be still. You are hurting my ears. All of your questions will be answered." Trevor blinked and found himself in front of his friend Josh's house.

"What are we doing here?" Just when he said that, Josh and Trevor ran in the house.

Trevor said "I remember this. This is when I got drunk for the first time. Why did you bring me here?" The man replied, "This is when you sold yourself to alcohol."

"It's not like I drink everyday," said Trevor.
"I only do it about once or twice a week."

Trevor then found himself at his house. "Why are we here?" he said. The older man pointed to a car swerving down the street.

"That guy is drunk," said Trevor, but as the car got closer he saw that it was himself in about five years.

"BANG!!" The car suddenly crashed into a telephone pole. Trevor ran over to it. He looked into the car. He was dead. He had died instantly with a broken neck. Trevor stood there motionless and speechless for about five minutes. When Trevor raised his head a tear came down the man's cheek. Trevor blinked again and they were on the trail. "I'll never touch that stuff again." "I know," the man replied as he vanished.

Trevor kept his word but often thought about what the man had said. "You are leaving, dying, and not free."

Writing In Literary Forms

It seems like only yesterday we shared the past.
Laughing together for hours. The tears we shed-
It seemed like enormous amounts of time passed
before we really knew each other.

As we stand along the river feeling lost and lonely
the memories (cutting flashbacks) continue.
Mom, it is easier to let go so you can
continue your journey to the other world.

I'll be alright.

Sitting here wondering just what you'd be doing.
Recalling our many visits of sharing and daring to care.
A strange fear paralysed us when we got too close.
Some things weren't dared discussed. Patience was
learned as I waited for those words unsaid

Time passed. Days. Months. Years. Patiently.
Those unsaid words some how left shadows on the past.
Love was in the room, felt strong although unsaid

Reminiscing I feel the loving flow in my heart, mind and soul
Serenity, for a second felt as our love-filled contentedness.
As I feel the memories then let them go. Soon there will be
serenity.
As I recall your departure, I got lost. For those words
not said, I can no longer ask.

A spark shines through the room full of love.
From your pride? Wonder flows as the spark brightens
The spark is so poignant as it pulls at my heart
As I reach out, reach and caress the spark, memories
start flowing as I pull the spark to my heart. Love
flows through and I can feel you in my mind, body, and soul

So I sit here and wonder what you're up to now?
Are you at peace? Are you happier? May the Great Grandfather
keep you filled with serenity.

Eddie LeRoche

Rainbows and Me

The many shades of vibrant
colour just after a sudden shower
Arching hi in the sky. It moves
along with you but you can
never touch it. Dorothy's song
"Somewhere Over the Rainbow"
Spectrum of light changing the
hue. Sprinkled with Fairy Dust
from Tinker Bells magic
Rainbow rides for lovers of life
A passage from the holy Book in
reference to remember, "a promise was made."
Sparkle of magic from the
Leprechauns shiny pot of gold
To believe it's special is to believe
in me.

I'm full of different hues
in colour like the rainbow
Sparkled with Tinker Bells
spirit for life. Remembering the
Promises I made. I'm rich because
I've held the Leprechauns pot
and my wishes are being answered
I'm special because I believe
in Rainbows and the places
over the Rainbow, yet my
sorrow that I hold can reach
the Rainbow.

It's magic
and it's free.

I Am

I am an aboriginal woman
who hurts and celebrates

I hurt for my people who are on the streets
homeless and begging for change
But I celebrate for my people
who are finding their path of life
gaining their pride once again

I am stil hurting from a past that haunts me
One of my sister and of my brother
kneeling in the snow on a cold winter night
begging for mercy to the cops
laughing in the cruiser

I celebrate because my mother took us away
so we could not see what happened next

I am still hurting
     I am still celebrating
I am healing

Olivia was two years old at the time of the incident with the police. Some things you never forget.

THE FIRST GRADE FIVE STUDENT IN MR. LAMPARD'S CLASS TO HAVE A (FUN) WEEKEND DETENTION

It was getting close to the end of the school year and everyone was misbehaving. Well, almost everyone was. There were lots of rumors going around like Linda loves Louie. People were getting into fights that didn't make sense, except for a few.

It was Friday afternoon and everyone was looking forward to the long weekend. All of the students were getting Monday off. Everyone except for Jeff, a student in Mr. Lampard's grade 5 class. Mr. Lampard had given Jeff a weekend detention. Jeff had to have a detention because he gave out all of the answers for all of the assignments to his classmates. Mr. Lampard was so fed up he decided to give the first weekend detention ever!

Then after school that day Mr. Lampard thought "what shall I make Jeff do for his punishment?" Mr. Lampard thought for a long time. He then he came up with a plan that would help Jeff see that giving answers to his friends is a nice thing to do, but it isn't the best thing for the others involved.

Well it was Saturday morning and Jeff had to go to school. As Jeff got ready for school he wondered what kind of punishment Mr. Lampard would give him. Would it be dictionary work or garbage duty? Well what ever it is Jeff thought he deserved it because he shouldn't have been giving out the answers. Well what ever the punishment was Jeff was ready for it even if it was 3 days of writing dictionary pages or picking up garbage. Jeff thought he deserved it. As Jeff approached the school he smelled the smell of pizza cooking. When Jeff got inside he found out that Mr. Lampard was cooking him pizza. Well maybe it wasn't going to be such a bad 3 days after all.

Jeff asked Mr. Lampard who the pizza was for and Mr. Lampard said,
"It's for you." Jeff was puzzled.

"I thought I have a detention?"
"You do!"
"Well why are you making me a pizza?"
"Because it is your detention."
"My detention! What kind of detention is this?"

"A fun one!" replied Mr. Lampard. Well all morning Jeff pigged out on pizza. Then for the rest of the day Mr. Lampard gave him sundaes. By 2:30 p.m. Jeff was stuffed. He went home and couldn't wait for Sunday because he was going to have gym all day. Also on Monday he would chew 20 packs of gum. By 2:30 p.m. Monday afternoon Jeff was so full and tired from having so much fun, and his jaw was sore from chewing all that gum. Jeff realized that the fun detention wasn't so much fun after all. From then on Jeff kept his answers to himself.

Kevin Henry

The Beach

It was time to head to the beach again. Every day from Monday to Thursday and sometimes Friday we would head down to the beach. There would be a lot of people going down and training in canoes. They would bring canoes and paddles down from the canoe shed and put the canoes and paddles near the water. They would take their shoes off and put their thongs or beach shoes on because the rocks are sharp and sharp barnacles stick to the flat surfaces of the rocks. The canoes would get put in the water and the people would get in and go for a little cruise. Then everyone would line up in front of the time keeper who would be seated on the beach. When the line was straight enough, the timekeeper would say go and they would be on a 15 to 45 minute training route. I would be seated on the beach with the sun shining in my face. I was throwing rocks constantly, while keeping my eyes on the canoes. The first canoe would go out of sight then the second canoe would go out sight then the third then the fourth and pretty soon the last canoes would be out of sight. I would pick up one more rock and throw it as far as I could. I would then head up to my favourite place where I would just sit there listen to the birds, see the fish jump, and hear the water rushing up onto the beach because of the waves of the boats.

The place I used to go to all the time was about twenty-five to thirty-five feet down the beach and up a hill from where the time keeper was sitting. I used to like going to this place because I would not be disrupted by civilization and I could hear the water rushing upon to the beach without really seeing it happen, but most of all I liked to see when the first canoe came in to where they first started off. From my favourite place, I could see each and every canoe come in one by one and also see who was paddling the canoe perfectly. When the last canoe came in I would leave my place until next time we went down to the beach again!

James, the Killer Whale

One day James was swimming around an island called Spiden Island. The island was very sacred to the Indians. James was a killer whale. James looked around the island for something to eat. He saw a seal about sixty feet away. He dove under water, opened his mouth and in one bite he ate the seal. He stayed around the island awhile. James was bored so he decided to go look for his pod. He was about a day behind his pod and swam as fast as he could. After awhile he got hungry again. He stopped to eat. After he ate, he went looking for his pod again. He had to stay away from the shore. If he went too close to the shore he might end up in an inlet or a bay. His mother always warned him about going too close to shore. He never paid attention to his mother and always wandered off somewhere and always ended up falling behind. After awhile James was tired of going fast and dove under water just for a little swim and when he came up he was in a little bay. James was wondering why everything was looking different, but didn't pay much attention.

He saw some seals and said "Gee, I haven't eaten in a long time." So he went and chased them. He ate. He tried to keep going but every time he would hit shore. Then he figured it out that he was in a bay and he couldn't do anything about it. He tried for a long time to get out but it got dark so he decided he would go to sleep.

When he woke up, he heard a horn. He found the noise. It was a fishing boat, and they were looking for a killer whale. They started to shoot harpoons at James but he dodged them and dove under water every little while. The fishermen were looking for him. He came right up against the boat. He heard one of the fishermen say, "Let's go put a net out so he can't get out." James thought if he followed the boat out it would lead him back out again. He was right. When he got out of the bay he turned around to look at the fishermen and they were still putting the net out. Just as he turned around there was his pod.

Alison Austin

FLYING

Flying up
Lady bug
Yellow plane
Insect
Noisy birds
Great owl

Vaughn Hedge Coke

MY FAVORITE PLACE

My favorite place to EAT
is my home.
           Because I like the
        taste of the food at my home.
My mom is a good cook,
she cooks the things I like.
It looks like roasted chicken and
stove top stuffing.
I love to eat in my room.

        Because it is quiet.

I like to eat at dinner time.
I like to eat on my
bed because it is comfortable.
        My room smells like it is clean.
          My room is dark.
       It sounds like EASY E on my cassette player.

I like to eat at home.

LIFE

If Death is an art,
then Life is a masterpiece
Don't waste your life on
something you can't have
Times have been hard
but you get through the pain
Joy is the Sunshine
But your dancing in the Rain
You think of the past,
and you let out a sigh
You think about the future
you then start to Cry
Things can be frightening
Bright as the Sun
or faster than Lightning
My point to you is that Life goes on
like an ugly scream
or a Beautiful Song.

Why Creator

I reach for the spirits,
I want to touch them,
I want them to touch me,
I want to dance with them.

I'm on Mother Earth,
I watch humans destroy,
I watch my brothers and sisters,
I watch them die.

I hear crying in the distance,
I hear a gun shot,
I hear a siren,
I hear a jail door slam.

I look around and ask
"Why Creator?"

Okijide Ikwe
(Woman Warrior)

Walking on crutches
laughing   crying   acting
wondering what happened
too many wrongs   too many mistakes
to actually remember
Watching lost warriors fight
unsure who our enemy is
Never realizing who friends were
watching clouds through bruised eyes
remembering visions given to us
forgetting their purposes
trying to erase memories
dark   violent   stormy
pasts
trying to build a distant future
when yesterdays are still relevant today
Walking on crutches
trying to act
moving
getting caught in red tape
Divide and Conquer just beginning
industrialist raping life of its beauty
telling lies to keep us quiet
Contradictions spreading in exploitation
beating equality rights to oblivion
conditioning the masses an illusionary thought
commercializing ways of life losing their depth
heartbeat fading
spiritual connections superficial
support being the judge and executioner
Child inside being brutally assaulted
never thinking what might have happened

Lawrence Angeconeb

Walking on crutches
looking through bruised eyes
grandmothers whispering in scarred lips
silent thunder sounding in chests around the world
broken legs organizing in masses
across burnt prairies stripped mountains concrete jungles
across the nation, an abused voice can be heard
healing
land   sky   water
crying   screaming   singing
I AM LIFE
I AM A MOTHER

I AM WOMAN

The Journey

Our skies aren't as blue
Our rivers aren't as clean
Though we are trying
The harder it may seem

We all have a road to follow
And ways to reach our goal
To make our ancestors proud
To make the circle whole

We need to recognize and restore
The future of our children
We need to realize the images
Our children see and feel
To complete the circle and keep it strong

We have to respect and know
The gift of woman
We have to teach our new generation
The power we have to complete
The circle within...each other

We just opened a new door
To our ancestral ways
Clearing our path once more
Clearing our eyes from the heavy haze.

Circle of Sunlight

In the circle of love's laughter
a child plays quiet sunlight
Mothers breasting baby suckles
winding blow

The autumn leaves, winter
hold tight man protecting
hands nurturing life
honour on one knee
the circle of sunlight

Travis Hedge Coke

HEADMAN
for Jack Conroy

He stands
no more than three years old
ordering older and younger children alike
"You go here." "You go fix that board!"
Voice loud as thunder
deep like
a full grown man
when he is older
He will be the Headman

Years pass by like fast cars
Still commanding
whoever listens
he's growing into his voice now
though it's still deep
He will be the Headman

Now he is six
he stands proudly
his voice deep
his words loud
they seem to defy his body
"I answer for Psa, Tasha, and Pierre."
he once said
His will strong
at least with most things
If you disagree with what he says
he will insure he gets his way
because when he is older

He will be the Headman

Someday he
will lead the people
but not today
now he will run and play
When he is older
He will be the Headman

but not today

When he is young
he will play

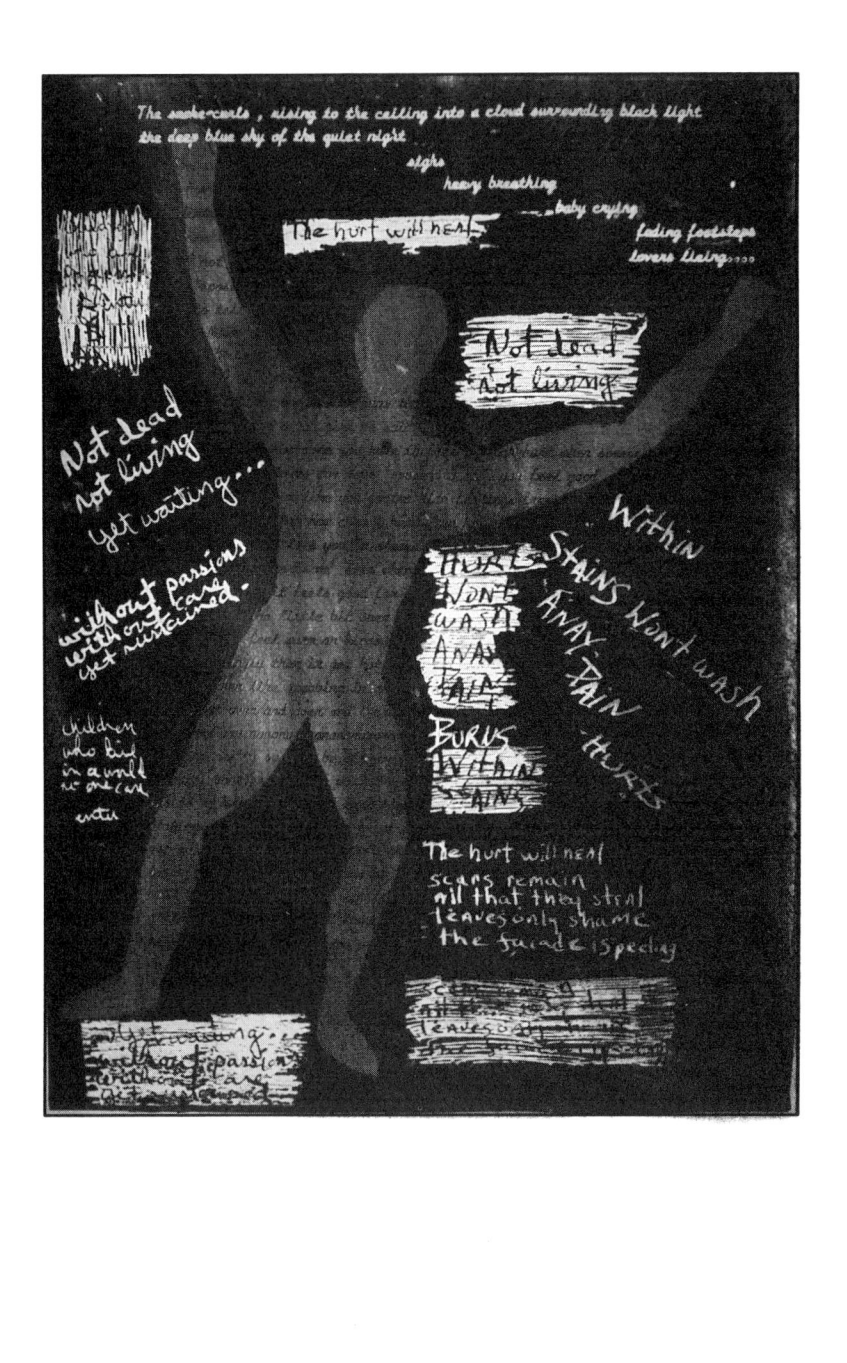

The smoke-curls, rising to the ceiling into a cloud surrounding black light
the deep blue sky of the quiet night
sighs
heavy breathing
baby crying
The hurt will heal
fading footsteps
lovers living......

Not dead
not living

Not dead
not living
yet waiting...

without passions
without fear
yet nurtured.

HURT
WON'T
WASH
AWAY
PAIN
BURNS
WITHIN
AIN

Within
STAINS Won't wash
AWAY PAIN
HURTS

children
who live
in a world
no one can
enter

The hurt will heal
scars remain
all that they steal
leaves only shame
the facade is peeling

Wind

Morningstar Mercredi

Long Wind Walk

Truth tastes putrid in a glass a mile long
like the last mile I walked in my skin so bronze clean
freshly painted the Mary Kay way defining who I want you to see
defacing Dances with Wolves stereotype-casted squaw with my
red lip stick second language of English but not by choice Blue
Nuns sliced my Mothers native tongue in the Residential School
then I lost myself on a journey towards Indianness where I was
introduced to a Messed up Medicine man who fondled my tits as
he doctored my spirit with his hands-on treatment along the trail I
met Wet Behind the Ears white guy who confused me with Immigration by asking if he fuck me to officially become a Canadian
seems you're not a real Canadian till you've had an Indian
woman he reminded me of a brown skin bro who told me Indian
women never say no shattering my mirror image with fragmented
pieces of stolen silence before I spoke I existed in their minds as
myths of something less than skinned meat left to rot on a
sidewalk

> *she stood on the corner waiting for the red light to give
> her permission to pass on the green, she was one of the
> most beautiful Indian women I've ever seen, I admired
> how she carried herself esteem, back arched straight,
> head as high as her exquisite cheek bones, bones with silk
> flesh beneath her jeans and Navajo blanket.*
>
> *she gave me pride...*

walking softly beneath blue skies my feet sliced open on broken
glass barricades of bullshit I cut in society my sanity hinged on
echoes of laughter as Lake Athabasca's shore tickled my youth
with wet kisses sharing innocence with loons who sang love songs
to me about the far cry from home skin would take me to find
myself missing moccasins shake the earth to the beat of one
pulsating breath of dust-filled laughter and song at the tea dance
in Dog Head back in the bush far away from hallucinations of
being Indian when survival was a pound of sugar lard flour and
tea when men hunted women gathered children giggled

she gave me a smile...

sweetly I sensed we shared a similar culture of instant soup, film, crazy T.V., computers, dreaming of vogue fashion, eating ice cream as life subjugated sexism and racism to our skin, despite a cast of reality she was a warrior with spiritual spunk walking in her era upstaged by past tense scribes, how many more decades before the silent screen would portray present day personalities of coherent strong Indian women whose characters cut their hair for fashion, paid taxes as long as the rivers flow, worked nine to five, related to the rebel in me who rides off on a Harley for the sheer pleasure of feeling free in my skin

she drifted into our culture...

our long wind walk would never end in our skin this comforting thought prevails me to count my blessings of sober solitude though drink killed the pain sheer existence and survival sucked my strength dry solutions break the silence of sexism celebrating sexuality shedding shame skin shedding shame skin

Russell Teed

My Voice

When I was young
too young to speak out
my mamma spoke the words for me
She'd ask me
Are you hungry?
She'd answer for me
Sure you are
She'd ask
Would you like breast milk?
She'd say
Sure you would
I couldn't speak
I'd cry
I'd cry out
No one listened
I didn't have a voice

When I learned my first words
my mamma put them in front of me
She put them in my mouth
She spoke the words for me
She'd say
Can you say mamma?
Can you say dadda?
I'd listen to her
She'd listen to me
say what she wanted to hear
I'd cry mamma
I'd cry out dadda
I didn't have a voice

When I was four
they took me away
They took my mamma from me
They took my dadda from me
They put new words in my mouth
They spoke the words for me

They'd say
Can you say new mother?
Can you say new father?
I'd listen to them
say what they wanted to hear
I'd cry mamma
I'd cry out dadda
I didn't have a voice

When I was sent to school
teachers taught me
what they wanted me to learn
They spoke the words for me
They'd say
Do you like French Science and Math?
They'd answer
Sure you do
They'd listen for me to
sound like them
At home I wanted to cry mamma
I wanted to cry out dadda
No one would have listened
I never had a voice

When I was sent to church
they washed my forehead
They washed my brain
They taught me what to pray
They spoke the words for me
They'd say
Do you believe in God?
They'd answer
Sure you do
They'd say
pray to our god
pray without a voice
They'd listen to the prayers
they wanted to hear
I wanted to cry mamma

Russell Teed

I wanted to cry out dadda
No one wanted to listen
I never had a voice

When I got older
old enough to speak my mind
they still spoke the words for me
They'd say to me
You're useless aren't you?
Sure you are
You don't know French Science and Math
Can't you do anything right
They taught me to hold my head low
I prayed
but not to their God
They'd say to me
Can't you even pray right?
I prayed again
but not to their God
I yelled Mamma
I yelled Dadda
I spoke the words for me
I had a voice

Sharron Proulx

she is reading her blanket with her hands

my son tells me that he writes depressing songs sometimes. people say to him that he must be depressed a lot. he says, no, that he's not. that he can't write when he feels down anyway. he says he just writes what he sees, man.

I like the way my son looks at things. for instance I very recently unrepressed my metisness. I'm metis. I used to say, "my mother was metis." I thought I wasn't because I'm white-skinned. I thought it would be rude to say I'm metis because I don't experience racism like my mother did. I'm not oppressed in the unrelenting way that aboriginal people are and I don't want to be accused of jumping on the minority bandwagon in order to appropriate other people's perspectives as a way of getting published. I think that would be cheesy and unethical.

my son looks at me and gives me his best knowing smile. he says, "mom, listen to what you're saying. metis means mixed blood, mom. you shouldn't have to be ashamed of who you are."

"you're right," I say. when my mom was a kid, the word was "assimilate!" my mom and all her brothers and sisters were fostered out into my dad's family. I didn't learn about my mom's family because nobody talked about them. they were all ashamed of that family. my grandfather (my mother's father?), they say he was a falling-down drunk who died because he froze himself up to his waist when he fell asleep in some gutter in the middle of winter. I've never even seen a picture of him. they say he was white, though. but then they said my grandmother was white too. she didn't look too white to me. I met my grandmother but not very often because after all she was a bad mother and she had her kids taken away from her by the children's aid. shameless, unnatural hussy, is what my father said.

my father was an evangelical white supremacist. I wondered why white skin was such an issue in my family.

a woman I know is metis. white skin was an issue in her family too.

Sharron Proulx

I knew her when she identified herself as "white." now she's a strong metis woman who's politically active in the aboriginal community. so I called her up and asked her if she'd share her story with me. she said my responsibility will be to the first people of this land first. that I'm a writer and an artist and so my job will be an important one. she said to find out who my metis grandmothers are. they'll help me to know what to do.

now, I took what she said very seriously. before I called her up I had this dream. in this dream I'm sitting on the right-hand side of a couch waiting for an appointment with someone. there's a briefcase lying flat on the floor near me and on top of it, also lying flat, is a small leather bag. it's in the shape of a briefcase too but it's small, about eight inches around. it's a golden tan colour with intricate weaving or beads or painting around the edges. I lean over to get a closer look at the bag and I feel a kind of physical feeling of its beauty, of the love in the hands that crafted it.

then I begin to see pictures forming on top of the bag and in the air above it. the pictures are three-dimensional, each one forming very slowly into focus and showing itself before changing its shape into the next. four pictures it showed, each in golden brown diaphanous light, like particles of sand.

then an elder comes out from an appointment and picks up both bags, one in each hand. the smaller bag starts to dance around in the air and pulls him about with it. he makes a "woahhhh!" sound and I say that the bag's been doing some pretty amazing things that it's been showing pictures. the bag pulls him to the floor and opens. its contents spill out onto the carpet. I realize it's a medicine bag and I feel I must hurry to help the man; is he okay?

yes he is he wants me to help him put the contents back into the bag. I start to collect his things into my hands and I get slivers of wood stuck into my finger tips. the slivers hurt a lot and they also feel to heal.

the elder's gone when I'm finished. he's left without his bag. I'm concerned about that and I close the bag and start to carry it away and to look for him.

a young man--husky, rough--blocks my way with the whole front of his body. I say in a strong voice to leave me alone I am a metis woman. he says he's a white man from some european country and he puts a knife to my stomach and says he'll slice me in half if I move. I don't move.

he keeps pushing at me with his body and his black clothes and I ask him what he wants but he just grunts and pushes at me. grunts and pushes at me.

across the way are three native women with a child and the women are weeping with despair. the child has left them and gone down a hill to die. the women call to me they want me to help them. I break away from the man and run past the women and down the hill. they're afraid to go down there because it's death down there and they're not ready for death. I'm able to reach the child and to carry her back up the hill. she's limp in my arms but she is moulded, moulds into me, and when I reach the top of the hill and the women, we all know that I've saved the child and that the child is in me. is me.

I hear some of my metis grandmothers when they talk to me now. one granny in particular. she says it's about time I started to hear her. her voice comes up from below smooth and warm. honey-soft. she's trying to tell me something. when I turn to look, she's gone. she starts to wear a little red knitted hat so I can see her. she's really very unromantic-looking. she's short and plump and she has no teeth. she laughs a lot and she's funny. I wanted to tell a funny story. some people tell me I have a good sense of humour. I think it's true too because lots of times when I say something people break out laughing.

a woman recently told me a funny story. she's metis, on welfare, and a single mom with four pre-school-aged kids. she asked me if I'd repeat this story whenever I had the chance because it's funny and it isn't just her story.

she said she didn't wear a bra. after she got married, it bothered her husband that she didn't wear a bra. suddenly her breasts were his concern. he worked with crass men, he objected. they made rude comments. could she please just wear a bra when she went out of the house? he even cried real tears. heartbroken. she'd almost forgotten why she didn't wear a bra. for sure her mom made her wear one when she was a teenager (whenever she could catch her). she'd decided sometime during puberty that no woman would've invented a bra. she looked it up in the library for sure. sure enough, some man had decided that women's breast needed hiding and hiking.

so, to please and appease this once passionate lover and now moody husband of hers, she began to wear a bra. most of the time. pretty soon he began to use her bra as an object of debasement. often, when he happened by, he would slip his finger under the elastic and snap it onto her skin, laughing loudly. then he began to deftly open the snaps here and there. when her breasts fell from their little lace prison, he'd grab at them from behind and squeeze them until the pain was unbearable. she told him this was painful and degrading to her. he would just laugh louder. "she used to love it when he coddled her breasts," he said. then he'd squeeze them even harder. "say daddy loves me, and then I'll stop. say daddy loves me and then I'll stop," he's say. having her back turned to this guy became a dangerous position to find herself in.

so eventually, she bought a bra with a frontal snap. when he began to open this bra (sometimes even in public), she realized (but was by this time five years, three-and-a-half kids into an abusive marriage) she realized she was trapped, just like her own sweet breasts. her husband's abuse was so subtle and so socially acceptable. he kindly pointed this out to her himself.

her husband became overtly abusive after her fourth baby was born. mentally and sexually, verbally and bodily. no bruises. no broken bones. very little outside contact.

she began to think of herself as lucky. lucky that he didn't beat her too badly when he raped. lucky to have food to eat. lucky to get a new pair of shoes. lucky to have an old beaten down second car.

lucky to go to the library. to be allowed to read. yes, even lucky to wear a bra.

I was very moved by this woman's story and I didn't think it was too funny.

"don't you get it?," she asks. "you don't, do you? ah well, that's okay," she says. "other women'll get it. do you at least know why I want you to repeat my story celebrating my beautiful braless breasts?"

my face is blank. she pats me on the back like I'm a child. "because I can," she laughs. "because I darn well can."

women don't tell too many funny stories. it isn't that funny things don't happen to women but women are pretty serious these days. we have to be anyway because who knows when we'll be cut off again. it starts slowly and at the level of poverty. lots of women there. one woman was cut off social assistance because they told her she had to get a job because her three kids were all in school now. they didn't ask too many questions and she killed herself anyway.

I don't see this world as a safe place for my kids to grow up in. and what about if they should decide to have kids? what'll be left for them? so often I find myself asking rhetorical questions or watching someone's disinterested middle-class gaze looking over my shoulder at some shiny thing or another.

a woman I know says she can't imagine what she'd do if she didn't have her parents to go to for money. me?, I can imagine having parents to go to for money, but I can't imagine what that would be like. she says her greatest fear is a fear of poverty. me?, mine's a fear of wealth. so how are we so different? I wouldn't advocate radical riches to rags, I tell her, but then there're so many things about people that I don't understand.

there're things about me that I don't understand too and trying to sift through how I became who I am is exhausting (though I never seem to tire from trying). maybe I'm an incurable narcissist and pretty soon I'll wake up one morning and I'll be a flower right there in my bed. my daughter will come into my room, see me the flower, and think, "oh, how thoughtful. mom must be gone out already and she's left this beautiful flower here for me to find. I think it's a tuberose because its scent fills the room and now it makes my nostrils flare. here, I'll just put it into some water. it's a desert flower so it'll last a while, maybe three weeks if it's fresh. I love the hollow stems. I think I'll pin it down later and start my own collection of dried petals, like mom has."

but then when she gets home from school, she may be a bit confused because the flower will have put herself back onto the pillow of my bed. she'll have covered herself up to her blossom and she'll be wondering how it is that she came to be who she is. she'll be wondering why she's still okay after having experienced the childhood she experienced. she wonders about that one a lot. she thinks that maybe repressing the most tender parts of her scent is what made her who she is.
she's still puzzled about having the ability to literally slow time down so that she can see and hear things in a slow and lazy way and then remember body language, words, details, that she knows very few people see or hear because they're busy being self-conscious or ambitious or some other self-centred thing. but her, she's mostly fluid when she goes from here to there she mostly listens and looks, listens and looks, but rarely does she shell her thoughts around her own. rarely does she censor past her skin her limbs her senses colours breezes that other people share.

this one gets to her the most. there's so much in the air that's missed. why can't they see? why can't they hear?

oh dear.

she wants to pull the blankets over herself and hide in there in the warm sweet darkness of her bed but then she remembers that no one will see her and no one will smell her and she has a job to do anyway. so she turns herself around and her petals are her silver hair and her hollow limbs they fill themselves with laughter.

MYSTERIOUS WOMAN

Who is she
coincidence we should meet
Where did she come from
what made her come out

Feelings of shared thoughts
fears, loneliness, and happiness
why did she appear suddenly
or was she always there

Trying to ask her "why do you appear before me"
I didn't hear a response
Without a sound
she sits and waits for another thought

A thought came to mind
will she direct me to a new path
that I tried to avoid following
or was this her thought
and her path

Feeling confused
unsure of what's happening
or was it her that was confused
about letting the world know who she really was

Questions
answers that are left untouched
but wait
she sees a vision of a young child
trying to hide her true feelings
about her outer thoughts

That vision was of her as a child
or was it of me through her eyes

Carrie Jack

As I listen to the flow of the water
splashing against the creek side
clashing against the rocks

Looking into the stream
life flowing before my eyes
I find my own reflection saying to me
"you are the mysterious woman"

You are the one who let the inner woman out
who desperately tried to stay hidden and mysterious

As I now stand here
gazing in the mirror before me
I can see the mysterious woman
unquestionable

I was the real woman inside
struggling so hard to be hidden from the real world

Now I have allowed myself to come out
of the hidden life
to a new and different society

Father, I am a woman now

Father--why did you leave me?
Why did you leave us all?
Three sons and a daughter
All different women--our mothers
Boy, you got around, Father.

How many women were there?
Did you love them all?
If you had so much love to go around,
how come there's none left for me?

And my brothers wonder too,
did you hold us, and rock us to sleep
or were you too busy
looking for more women
to make more babies with?

And why didn't you leave me
a sister?
How many X's and Y's
you must have had
raging in your body.

Did you trust that our mother's
would care for us even though
you weren't here?
I guess you knew we'd
turn out alright.

I'm not mad, Father;
only curious.
I miss you, Father.

I miss being sung to sleep
with Eskimo songs.

I miss eating seal and walrus
caught by your harpoon.

Cheryl Ann Payne/Kylee Bautnuq Punguk

I miss cutting fish you caught
in your net
and driving across the bay in your boat.

I miss going to fish camp
and picking berries.

I miss stories of Rocky Point
and how you can tell the ice is rotten
the mountain.

I miss you telling me ghost stories
and taking me up to hot springs
up Fish River.

Or up to the timbers
to see the Golden Eagles.

Well, Father,
you left when I was only
a baby;
so I didn't know you.

Can I ask you to come to me in
my dreams
and tell me secrets
of being
Eskimo?

Will you whisper in my ear
that
you love me?
That you will watch over me
from the secret place of death?

Will you promise me
you won't ever leave
my memories?

Cheryl Ann Payne/Kylee Bautnuq Punguk

And will you whisper to me
about your life
I never hear about?

I have only heard about
your drinking.

And how you might have
killed a man.

And how you were in the stockade for
wanting to defect to Switzerland.

And how you used to hit your women.

Boy, you had a temper, Father.

You must have passed that on to me.
But aren't there other things of me
that are like you, too?

Please let me know, Father.
I don't want to be half monster.
I want to be loved,
by you, Father.

Please come to me in my dreams,
Father.
Help me understand why
you lived your life the way you did

Please, Father, let me know
it will be alright.

I am a woman now,
Father.
Do you see me
and are you proud?
Father, I love you.

Why?

Tell me why I don't know.
My ignorance is a loss,
Something that could have been.
It died in me, before I was born.
Who can tell me why I don't know?

Mother...?
    Grandmother...?
        Great-grandmother...?

    WHY?

I hate that word.
But half-breed describes me so well
I only feel like half.
I am half of a person
Half of an Indian
With only half of a soul.
I am accustomed to your rejection
If you don't refuse me
I will do it to you.

Oh Mother!
Come back to me.
I need to know,
I need to learn,
Learn with me, dear Mother
I feel so alone, so blind and dumb
I want to learn, but where are the tools?
Where were they hidden? Where are they now?

Like her, I am scared
It is difficult to rebuild
And then be destroyed by rejection
Sometimes,
It is my own rejection.
I am not strong enough

I am not ready.
I WANT MY MOTHER!

Yes,
Okay.
I will learn for both of us.

It does not matter why.
Plan for how.
Close the door on past hurt
If not, let it strangle
What hurts more?
Look forward,
Towards the power that may be?
Or dwell
On what cannot be changed?

For her,
For us,
I shall rebuild the circle,
Make us whole.
I will find strength in her memory.
To take the path of renewal
I do not walk alone
There are many who walk beside me.

I thank you.

Mary Lawrence

STANDING AT THE CROSSROADS

Marina died a lonely death on September 27, 1987, in a quiet room at the Intensive Care Unit in the hospital. The nurses failed to retrieve her after another alcohol seizure. Marina's hand was buckled to the bed railing during her final attempts of clinging for more breaths.

I am deeply moved by her death, not only because she was my cherished friend, but the mysterious events that surrounded her drinking. Marina had nine-and-a-half years of continuous sobriety. She was cheerful, bright and lively, always encouraging me to try her way of life; however, I had not hit enough bottoms yet. Still trying to wipe out the pains of my unhappy past, I drank until the ritual of taking pills and washing down the sadness nearly led me to a lonesome grave. Finally, I was able to put "the plug in the jug" and get sober.

Marina, an attractive, proud Blackfoot Indian, came from the Blood Reserve in Alberta. She was stocky and stood about five feet six inches. She had dark brown eyes and a dazzling smile. She looked much more youthful than her 47 years and always stood out in a crowd by wearing fashionable outfits with matching accessories. Her personality was filled with bursts of spontaneous laughter and gaiety. Her warmth attracted many who became close friends.

When Marina started boozing the progression of drinking consumed her for three years. My friend hit a lot of bottoms - spiritually, emotionally and physically. She'd drink and then she would stop. Off and on, her relapses were almost parallel to the number of years she had in sobriety. Ironically, during those three years she had about nine relapses and each one was unbelievable. To this day, I'm still amazed! It's almost like God gave her nine lives and still thirsty, she plunged into destruction.

In the last year of Marina's drinking, on a cold blistery evening in January when I was only a month sober, I was thinking about drinking as I drove around. Instead, I travelled along Highway 33 toward Marina's secluded home. It seemed like I was being guided there and before I knew it I was driving down the street near her house. An ambulance was parked in her driveway. The flashing red lights caused me to become panic-filled. I rushed inside and found Marina held down by two paramedics as they tried to tighten the restraints on the stretcher. There was blood spurting from her mouth, yet she still struggled for release. I assured her that everything would be all right and I would be following the ambulance right behind her. In living colour, I relived my own personal experience as I gaped at her. It had always been hard to visualize my recent stay in the hospital. I bled profusely from the nose, mouth and rectally from a ruptured stomach caused by excessive drinking and abuse of prescription drugs. Seeing Marina this way quickly removed thoughts of drinking I had earlier. I thanked God for my new-found sobriety and sped to the hospital, wiping away tears and praying for Marina's life.

During that night, I sat by Marina's bedside, staring with wide-open hopeful eyes, comforting her. I helped the nurse to hold her down each time she had another alcohol seizure. Unbelievably, Marina pulled through. Eventually, she got strong enough and left the hospital. She stayed sober for almost three months, living life to its fullest.

Unexpectedly, I dropped in to visit her one afternoon and tears welled up in my eyes as I gaped upon her. This time she lay in her crumpled bed, almost blind. She kept reaching for her bottle of beer but couldn't find it. As I sat by her bedside she begged me to give her a beer. Unwillingly I took the opened bottle of stale beer from the bed stand and placed it in her hand. I told her she did not have to drink and there was a better way. I did not want her to have that beer, yet knew she would get it, regardless. I placed a blanket on the carpeted bedroom floor and reached for a pillow. I lay there beside her and during the night got up and called the ambulance a couple of times. Help was denied. The dispatcher said they were unable to send anyone because Marina had refused to cooperate whenever an ambulance was sent. She continued to take sips of stale beer during the night and the next morning I returned home, unable to help her in any way.

Several days later, Marina partially regained her sight. She had called a cab and was heading out to replenish her supply of booze when she fell on her front steps. Because her body was losing its potential to fight off infection, the cuts on her leg from the fall became swollen and infected. Following another trip to the hospital for detoxification, the doctor also warned her it was certain her leg would have to be removed. Despite the doctor's warning, Marina left the hospital and continued to drink at home. One night, a small group of concerned Christian friends came to her house and vigilantly prayed over her. A miracle happened. Gradually Marina's leg healed, although she still needed to use crutches for awhile. Her sight improved too but she continued to drink.

Over the next few months Marina and I slowly grew apart. We didn't talk on the phone as much and I knew I had to associate with people who were alcohol free in order to stay sober myself. The odd time I phoned Marina to see how she was doing. Sometimes she'd pass out still holding the phone.

One Friday night, I joined a small group of sober people for an evening out of dancing and drinking cokes. I still enjoyed the odd night out. In the disco, I spotted Marina, sipping on a cocktail in a dark corner of the crowded night spot. She didn't notice me but I felt saddened to see her wavering on the stool as she sipped from a goblet of booze.

Summer had come and gone. It was nearing the end of September. Around eleven-thirty one night, I received an unexpected telephone call from Marina's daughter, Tracy. She said she had been to the hospital earlier and her mom was in bad shape and asked me to go to the hospital right away. I jumped in my car and rushed into town, speeding on the dark highway. I stopped long enough to pick up my closest friend, Morag, who had been sober quite some time. Shortly, we arrived at the hospital. Marina looked grave. I turned to Morag, looking for some assurance. She responded, "She knows we are here. All we can do is pray for God's will." We stayed at her bedside for quite some time until Morag suggested we go home, wait and pray. I phoned Tracy when I got home and assured her, her mom was going to be okay.

Early the next afternoon, I went to visit Marina again. This time she was sitting up, talking with Tracy, eating a fresh orange, laughing and looking much better. We had a nice visit and upon leaving her I told her I'd be over to visit her at her house in a few days.

Unexpectedly that same evening, I received another phone call from Tracy. Frantically, she asked me to come to the hospital right away. I rushed into town and felt chills go up and down my spine during the quick drive along the deserted highway. Marina was now in the Intensive Care Unit. I met Tracy in the small waiting room on the second floor. She looked so worried. Quickly, Tracy buzzed the intercom and the nurse released the locked double doors. Because Marina had specifically requested my presence, the nurse didn't question if I was a family member before letting me into the intensive care unit. Inside, Tracy's dad was pacing the floor in front of the nurse's station, directly adjacent to Marina's room. In the bed, Marina lay, wrenching in pain. Her face looked all twisted and yellow. It seemed that the fatal malady of alcoholism had launched its teeth into her and was slowly chewing her bit by bit. I stood by her bedside, wiping her face with cool cloths and placing paper trays at her disposal as she filled them endlessly with blood spurting from her nose and mouth. Tracy stood nearby, grief-stricken. When it was unbearable for her she'd leave the room. Marina spoke the odd time. Once she said, "I'm so tired, I just want to go to sleep." She told me she was afraid and I asked her if she still believed in God. She said, "Yes, I do." She then began asking for a minister and close family members. I assured her everything was going to be all right and that she was in God's hands and to hang in there. I was certain she would pull through. Shortly, the chaplain was called to her bedside. The nurse had also called their family doctor to come immediately.

It was well past midnight and Marina had settled down a little. Tracy and I went downstairs to quickly get a coffee, expecting it to be a long night. At the coffee machine we bumped into the family doctor as he was leaving. In passing, he informed us Marina was "on her way out." He didn't comfort Tracy. He seemed to be in a hurry to get home. We dashed toward the elevator and went upstairs to her room. The nurse was standing at her bedside, turning off the machine that had measured her irregular heart beats. Tracy's dad stood nearby, silent and sad. At 1:07 a.m. Marina's struggle had ended. She transformed into a beautiful ashen colour and her lips became soft, silky and glazed. I stared at her. Tracy was beside me, holding back tears. We stood for a long while. When the nurse covered her with the sheet we left the room. As we stood at the front entrance of the hospital I told Tracy she was a pillar of strength for what she had just been through. I hugged her and left her standing there as she waited for her dad to come down. I drove home, utterly shocked, hurt, mystified and angry that her own doctor could be so cold-hearted.

Five days later we attended Marina's funeral. It was very sad. Her wake was held at her house and many of her family from the Blood Reserve attended. We all reminisced of how she had touched each one of us with friendship, loyalty and love. In the bedroom, her husband Alex neatly folded her clothes and put things in the drawers. Still in shock, he mused how Marina liked to go shopping and would probably like to wear a certain outfit he held up, clutching a matching pair of earrings in the other hand. The few of us who were in the bedroom agreed on what Alex had decided she would wear. It was a long, beautiful peacock-blue dress. We were amused at how he could light-heartedly reflect on her perfectionism for matching clothes and accessories. No one person scorned Marina for having drunk too much; everyone could identify with her disease of alcoholism and sympathized.

Today, I accept the death of my beloved friend and I understand it was God's will to take her out of her suffering because Marina could not find continuous sobriety anymore. I am assured her resting place was pleasant and her final journey was peaceful because she surrendered and put her life in God's hands to take her out of her misery. As I reflect, her memory still lives inside me gracefully. Nearing my seventh year of sobriety I strongly believe Marina's experience is a strong reminder of what could happen if I ever decide to pick up a drink or pop a pill. Her memory will stay vividly etched in my mind forever. I miss her.

Graveyard
for Gabriel, and many others

WIDE SHOT
-back in the CORNER
the suicides -[1]

EXTREME CLOSE UPS, WHITE CROSSES
(shot gun)   April 20, 1973 - December 12, 1991
(hanging)   June 2, 1975 - August 3, 1990
(overdose)   June 18, 1969 - January 27, 1989
(shot gun)   February 2, 1972 - December 16, 1990
(sniffing)   March 14, 1974 - February 18, 1992
(sniffing)   December 12, 1975 - February 18, 1992.
(hanging)   July 23, 1976 - July 27, 1993.
(peanut butter) August 7, 1975 - May 16, 1992

        DISSOLVE

*B&W, RED TINT

WIDE SHOT
The TV is on in a large living room.

SOUND UP, GNR
in   the   jungle
W E L C O M E
to   the   jungle

b   r   i   n   g
you   to   your
K N E E S

K N E E S
K N E E S
K N E E S

[1]**MEMO**
TO: John Harris, Executive Producer
FROM: Maureen O'Connel, Executive Assistant
Sorry to report - costs of sending the seven-person crew from Toronto exceeded budget estimates by $11,014. Price of food was higher than expected, and camera broke down - took five extra days for replacement to arrive. Crew are 'glad to be home.'

K N E E S
K N E E S [2]

MEDIUM SHOT
Young Indian boy turns the TV off,
pours a cup of tea, and sits on couch

CLOSE UP, HAND
Takes the silver and turquoise ring off his left hand
CLOSE UP, WRIST, SLO-MO
Takes the medic alert bracelet off his left wrist
CLOSE UP, NECK
Takes the beaded buckskin thong from around his neck

AUDIO 2 TRACK - ABORIGINAL DRUMMING
Observes the beaded buckskin thong
for several minutes

MEDIUM SHOT
Spreads Kraft Extra Crunchy
on a piece of bannock

EXTREME CLOSE UP, EYES
Observes the sandwich
for about three minutes

DISSOLVE

*****FULL SCREEN - KEY RED**
ABORIGINAL VOICE-OVER [3]
mind sped up like a video fast cut blurrin like water rushin thru the dam rushin endlessly powerfully constantly if u put yr hand into the stream u feel the water poundin poundin with force pushin u pushin around u desperate to envelope u make u go away i dunno i cannot tell what they are thinkin i cannot tell what they are thinkin about me they occasionally acknowledge me with a glance nd i'm thinkin do they think i'm stupid dumb a plague i dunno bein ignored like i should be doin more more pretty more smart more funny i need

touch i want to touch i can't touch anyone yr touch there's no tenderness i don't know them well enough to touch them breakin free breakin free free free i dunno all i feel restless distracted cannot concentrate on anythin but how much power is in my limbs angry power drivin very very very fast with poundin beat of music tryin to relieve the

[2]**MEMO**
TO: Maureen O'Connel, EA to EP
FROM: William Brown, Director of Music Programming
Maureen, I just wanted to inform you that using Guns "N Roses Welcome to the Jungle could cost as much as $6200. Is anything Canadian possible? It's far cheaper, and CanCon helps when CRTC time rolls around.

[3]**MEMO**
TO: Maureen O'Connel, EA to EP
FROM: Barney Singh, Talent Director
As per your request, I have faxed the voice-over script to agencies of Graham Greene, Tom Jackson, and Gary Farmer. Could I suggest that it may be very expensive to procure their services, and that we audition for some fresh talent?

tension tryin to relieve the tension relievin the tension in every part of my body especially my mind my mind wantin to be free on the highway free in the bush effortless in the water soarin in the sky like   Nanabush

    DISSOLVE

*B&W, RED TINT

REPEAT, SLO-MO
Spreads Kraft Extra Crunch
    onto a piece of bannock

    DISSOLVE
*COLOUR

CLOSE UP
Takes a bite of sandwich

duncan mccue

WIDE SHOT
- dead on the FLOOR
in fifteen minutes -

**AUDIO 2 TRACK - ABORIGINAL DRUMMING
FADE UP, WHITE CROSS**

Donny Robert Goosecalls
August 7, 1975 - May 16, 1992

      FADE TO BLACK

            SUPER
*Assistance provided by
the Department of Indian Affairs
and Northern Development*

INSERT MOLSON CANADIAN COMMERCIAL[4]

---

[4]**MEMO**
TO: Maureen O'Connel, EA to EP
FROM: Heather Petrosky, Director of Advertising Revenue
Mau - Confirming that both DIAND and Molson's have pulled funding. Both believe the piece is projecting 'a negative image.' John may have to re-consider the focus.

UNTITLED

no definition
only glimpses
of the whole;
hazel eyes,
sandy hair,
tall, lanky,
cowboy hat.
she was dark;
black eyes and hair
warm, brown
in love
far from home.

cowboy and indian girl
it's not clear
how they met
it's almost funny
(in a hollywood
kind of way)
to imagine
saddening
to realize
a man would
deny his child
his name
rarely spoken
his antics
the same
a gift of canned pears
his underwear thrown
out the window
how a best friend
lusted for him
and left us to die.
this is all i know...

Debby Keeper

---

i asked of her
how am i named
"after a movie star"
was the answer
oh how i have been shamed.
i seek knowledge
of the other self
that looks like me
(yet somehow not the same).

definition;
english speaking
mixed blood;
father,
caucasian
irish
cowboy;
mother,
cree
a little bit
scottish;
grandmother,
cree
partly
scottish;
grandfather,
adopted
believed to be
cree
maybe some
saulteaux
this is all i know.

WHERE WERE THE WOMEN

Where were the women
when, you put your
X
on the dotted line?
Surrendering our lands
"as long as the
sun shines above
and the waters
flow in the ocean."

Where were the Kohkums
when, you ceded released surrendered
and yielded up to the
Government, of the Dominion of
Canada
all our rights
titles
and privileges?

Where were the mothers
when you the Chiefs and Headmen
traded away our future
one square mile for
each family of five
twelve dollars
powder shot calico
and other articles?

Where were the daughters
when, the said Indians
entered into agreements
with the Great White Mother
solemnly promising
to conduct and behave themselves
as good and loyal subjects...
to strictly observe the Treaty?

Where were the women?

Janice Acoose

We Are Sensual/Sexual, Happy/Beautiful, Strong/Powerful People Too

Have you ever seen healthy, smiling faces of Native peoples in love, Native couples so completely immersed in each other's love? Have you ever seen brown skin loving brown skin, Native lips kissing other Native lips in television, film, video, or the many different forms of print?

Its pretty safe to say that most people have not. I know I have never seen images of my self--as a Native woman--represented in any medium as a happy, healthy, sensual/sexual being capable of love and being loved by a man from my own culture.

What does the absence of loving/sexual Native images communicate about ourselves, to our children, to others outside our cultures? If we cannot see representations of ourselves as loving, healthy, sensual/sexual Native peoples in books, magazines, films, videos, and television, are we suggesting that we are not loving, happy sexual beings?

A short time ago I happened to look upon my son and his white-blue-eyed-blonde girlfriend as they shared a very intimate moment. I watched as he lovingly held her face in his hand, kissed her and held her close to him. I was so moved by the depth of his feelings for her.

Sometime later I asked him, "why don't you or your brother ever date Native girls?" Even before the last words came out of my mouth, I knew. I thought of all those Cindy Crawford, Claudia Schiffer, Madonna type pin up posters that adorn my sons' walls. That's when it hit home: Native girls/women -- even with our wonderfully alive brown beautiful skin -- we don't fit the ideal beauty myth. And, young impressionable boys and men want to love and be loved by girls and women who most closely resemble that ideal beauty myth.

The absence of images of ourselves as attractive, happy, healthy, sensual/sexual beings tells me that we are not worth loving. That we are incapable of loving each other!@ It also tells me that we cannot be romantic or sexual with each other, that there's something wrong or even perverse in desiring each other's bodies.

We've certainly seen enough images of ourselves as unhealthy, unhappy, unwhole, and dysfunctional peoples. Oh, and yes, we've seen images of the white woman/Native man or Native woman/white man romantic combination, which usually ends in disaster and more often than not as a result of the Native person's seemingly inherent character flaw.

As Native peoples, we talk so much about restoring ourselves to balanced respectful beings. We call upon that oh-so-tiresome word "heal" to remind us of our pain and misery.

We need to remember that we have happiness, beauty, strength, power, sensuality, and sexuality in our cultures too. We need to construct those kinds of images through our art, music, and other kinds of cultural reminders of ourselves.

I know that some Native people are struggling to represent those aspects of our cultures through their work. Unfortunately, I'm too often reminded that publishers, filmmakers, and producers are just not interested in love stories about healthy, happy Native peoples. I've surmised that White audiences therefore are only interested in us when we're hurting each other, killing one another off, or suffering from alcoholism or drug addiction. Isn't that the most powerful propaganda that keeps us disempowered?

Jim Logan

you're beautiful

you said, you thought i was crazy
'only half', i lied
'and watch out 'cause
i believe it's catchy
and once you've got it
there's no place to hide'
then the room filled with thunder
that rolled from the heart beats
that rushed up through veins in shattered hands
that pulsated over your feathered breasts
and i wanted to make love to you
and i wanted you to love me
and i had all my reasons
bound in a worn out parfleche
but the morning sun
clouded all my intentions
and all the drinks i swallowed
came at once to haunt me
like ghosts from old christmas trees
and i fought with the spirits
(yours were there too)
and my mind was in turmoil
taking me from lust to love
from the garden to the cross
from my loved one to my promise
i didn't want to care, but did
(and i believed so did you)
and with my craziness confirmed
we let it all rest
and when it came time to leave
there at Winnipeg airport
a 'you're beautiful' was all....was all,
i could attest

hero

may 18th, i find myself
strangely wanting to be with you
for reasons only i would know
and i desire to parade down queen street
and to lift a drink
to old friends, old loves still in tow
and to stay with you through the night
and to dream and float amongst mystic medicine wheels
despite the noise of the city below
so i phoned, only to say 'how ya' doin'?
and answered 'the wife and kids are fine
but the paintings are goin' slow'
and i never gathered the courage
to say the words i wanted to say to you
that came to me, so clearly, only a moment ago

oh, how i wanted to give you ribbons
bright in colour and full of honour
for you to wear wherever you'd go
and i wanted to enter your mind galloping on a wild pony
with my face painted and my wounds exposed
showing myself off as your typical plains cree hero
ha! what craziness is within this desire
what dreams flash and fade with your presence
and what scant memories i have to stow
of my dear friend who stayed with me
that night i drank too much
in the vast loneliness of toronto
yeah, there are days my friend
i miss your company, your protection
and there are reasons for this that only i know

Sarah Lyons

Sense and No Sense

Who needs food when the sun comes out?
I'll just eat this gentle wind
and chew on the vision of this flower

pink collar blues
rust & caring
beg sentimental tears

in the shadows--educatee's educator
in the shadows--softness and a hum
fuzzy vision & a toothache
carrot seeds lost in the soil

in the shadows--comfort
in the shadows--a turkey hunt
lambs brae
the smell of wet wool and soaking pastures
hoof sucking the saturated field
stamping in horse & rider

in the shadows--the sun comes out
body parts floating up at Lincoln beach
my sisters raising children

in the shadows
a vacant tenderness
smile & kiss
spreading fingers
before the first
reluctant shadow
dragging along
sense & no sense
drinking a song

in the shadows
a vacant tenderness
smile & kiss
spreading fingers
before the first
reluctant shadow
dragging along
sense & no sense
drinking a song

Marcia Crosby

Speak Sm'algyax Grandma, Speak Haida Grandpa

Dear Gram:

I am writing you too long after you are gone. But never so gone that I do not weep your absence and miss your voice. I was wondering if you were wondering how I was doing? Do you know that I went to university and got a degree? and now I am getting another one--a Master of Arts they call it. They say it's important to have this piece of paper because it will give me the way, the passage, the ticket, the language to tell my story. But grandma, I wonder if you really want me to tell my story. You see I learned about why and where the night and pain and all of the things that you would not let us speak about came from. I learned about what happens to people, like grandpa, when they're sent to residential school. In university, there's nothing in the textbooks that say anything about who we are. I mean gram, we go to school to learn about them and when they think we can think like them and speak like them, then we get a degree. But even though I know how to speak and act like them, I am like you. I am not sure if I can speak and I don't know if it's okay to speak, to tell the story of our pain, to talk about the abuse of our people and why grandpa abused me.

Did you know gram? Did you know that the pancakes he cooked us in the morning were part of the nightly ritual of visiting me in bed in secret in the dark? Did you know that the good smells were a lie? Did you know that my morning baths couldn't make me feel clean? The water, rocking the boat, the boat where he abused me, where he led me to the galley and into the engine room. Did you know that after I walked down the wharf onto the boat and entered that voyage of self-hatred cloaked in family smells and nurturing sounds that I knew you knew? It makes me feel dead inside oh so so tired. Yes nights, nights, and rocking. Rocking alone downstairs by myself. No hands to cradle me, no soft palms to wipe away my fear, no tears, just me rocking, empty and alone with my fear that I was a pregnant eight year old. So so alone, so alone that I remained there, too alone to name my fear and speak the act. Semen sliding down my leg in the middle of the night, too afraid to move, lying still waiting and waiting waiting to slide down the wall waiting to disappear into the darkness. Jesus Christ. how long do I have to be alone? When is it alright to tell my family, my community? I was raped over and over, over and over.

Say fondled. No...abused. No...touched. No. Not raped. Don't say the word, he made you pancakes in the morning. He made you pancakes and he was so quiet when he touched me. Not a word, not a threat, not a sound, just heavy breathing and grunting and touching. And silence. I am so quiet in this world. I will not be silenced. I write now using a huge Webster's dictionary like the one he used to use for cross-word puzzles. Grandpa was so smart. he always used that great big dictionary. he learned a lot at the residential school.

When I wake up in the morning I sometimes think this is the day to die. Death, inevitable when I think I am all alone in this world with my pain and I wish somebody could fix it because I don't know how. Maybe that wish is like when I was a little girl and I used to dream about saving all the poor dirty kids standing outside the bar waiting for their parents. I wanted to take them home and bathe them in the tub that you used to bath us in. I think about being clean and being loved and I wish I could clean up the whole world with that same gesture of love that we experienced in the morning in our tub. Did you think you were washing away the night of abuse? Did you think it would wash away the secret and your silence? I don't know grandma but my faith in the need and the ability to truly clean the world up with a bath is an act of love that ignores life's ugly realities. This is not something I want to do. I want to love the way you did but not in pretended ignorance. I want to love but not in silence. I want to speak the night and speak your gesture of love. I want to speak, to scream, to wail, and to cry out, yet, I need to dance, to heal myself. I want to expose the night so we can have our day.

When I write, I dance my words on the page. I speak sadness with the joy of self-realization, of agency and self-identity. I am whole even in my fractured life of so many worlds: the village, the city, my colleagues, my children, and my family. Oh god I just want to dance. I just want the world to flow out of me. I just want my joy to be true. But it's so rare so far away. let my joy be true. Let it last a little longer next time. At times when I think life is pretty good for me as an Indian woman like right now this moment as I speak to you, I take the words, and dance them on the page. But then my

Marcia Crosby

Indian woman/child surfaces and is angry and frightened and tired and sad. I work hard to put the punctuation where it belongs (belongs?) to make her dance to make music for her but the form will not produce the Marcy of childhood, of my young womanhood. I can only dance her with the language that I have now. I hardly remember the joy of childhood. And the times when I experience the satisfaction of being able to write/dance, I must always speak of the abuse of power. When will I dance truly joyfully? I want to write about me dancing for you, scarf whirling around spinning, you laughing, remember? I want to write about the possibility of empowerment, agency, happiness and potential for Native women while she dances. I think that if I keep writing the world that it might happen. But how? Where do I find the strength to continue? It's there in your love grandma. The bath, laugh behind the soft palm, the gentle proddings.

Go ahead and dance; no one will laugh at you except with delight that you are Marcy, this girl who we nurtured to speak our silence. We cannot speak we cannot tell the secret. Speak for us Marcia. Dance, we will watch and encourage you with our hearts, forgive us for not speaking; we could only teach you. We could only give you partial joy and let you realize the rest your self. We are so sorry we could not say the words to make the night go away. We could only love you in the daylight; it is up to you now to speak the night. We will love you even if other people don't want to hear your words. We will love you because we brought you up to speak, to dance the rest of the story.

Grandma, I want to dance for you again. I want the joy, the self-confidence of dancing for an audience of love. A self with the promise of a future. To become that same child who emerged from time to time despite the pain. I want to tell of the joy I feel when I speak words that come from all the nuances of your love and murmurings, ah shah, don't cry dear. I want those soft palms that dried my eyes and gentle rocking to mix with this language I've learned in school. I want the caring you had for our family, our community to meld with my text. I want to tell them our story, the one you gave me with songs and stories of the porcupine and the beaver. Remember when you washed us in the tub every morning grandma and then gently combed our hair? I can only speak of abuse. I want to tell the story of love.

Oh Marcia, forgive me for not speaking. I could not let my self realize the pain.

I can hardly speak your words because I think you might not forgive me for telling the story you wanted to keep a secret. Yes, some of our leaders, some of our old people and others in our communities want us to be quiet about life on our social and geographical reserves. They want us to be silent and if we are not then we are not family. But your silence deadened me, gram. This is about love and anger. This is about sadness and joy. About strength and the total collapse of the spirit.

It is up to you to speak the night. It is up to you to tell the story of your and our abuse.

It's up to me to speak, to speak the night. I must speak the night of a colonial history that overlaps with the reality of my own night that continues into day. To tell Grimm's fairy tale of colonialism. Will I ever speak it so that people will be compelled to listen to a storyteller? I speak the night with pain and with reluctance but if I don't, I will die.

Why did the porcupine leave the beaver up in the tree? Tit for tat, that's what you get. No big mystery about an old Indian story that sounds more like an Aesop's fairy tale.

I think about what you taught us. How to be white with Indian stories, drinking tea from a cup and saucer and not a mug. Oh gram this is such confusion such pain. I wish you could have said to me you are Tsimshian and our clan is Gisbutwaada, Killer Whale and our people came from a strong matriarchal society. I am teaching you the way of all of your grandmothers. I want you to grow up big and strong like all the great matriarchs in our family. But gram you didn't say it. You couldn't say it. Instead you were silent while your husband abused me. You could only pass on the love of nurturing me in a bath tub. Did the missionaries teach our people we could wash away the dirt of being Indian? Where on earth was all of the knowledge of our grandmothers? I want it. I don't want to have to decipher this cryptic code of love and self-loathing in search of some kind of Indian self identity. It would have been so easy if you could have spoken the world in Sm'algyax. I am crying for us because someone took the language of our grandmothers and replaced it with English, tea in a cup and saucer and such good manners that we could not speak the sickness that happened in our night. Such good English manners that we did not cry rape rape RAPE. STOP.

We are nations of women and men who love our children. We are nations with chiefs because our families eat together at our feasts. What if we gave a feast and nobody came? Help me to tell them gram. Turn your face first towards your children. Speak Sm'algyax. Speak Haida. Gently. To us, your families, and then we will speak as nations. Big chiefs. Big names. Big words for white people don't comfort children at home. Oh gram. How could you be silent? To hell with their manners. To hell with their world. Speak Sm'algyax, speak Sm'algyax.

Speak Haida, grandpa. Speak the language they told you not to speak in residential school. Speak the language of family you could not learn in a school without mothers and fathers and aunties to tell you how to behave. Where they tried to teach you to be like them before you could learn how to love your unborn grandchildren. If you speak Haida, grandpa, will the silence of abuse be over? If you speak our own language will you remember who you are? Speak Haida, grandpa, speak Sm'algyax, grandma. So we can be a family, be a community, be strong nations of people. Speak to one another first. Sing our own songs and dance our rights and privileges with honour and love. I want to dance with my own people. It's time to dance with you grandma and grandpa. Time to dance with my daughters, and my son.

So I have to go now. I will miss you as I always do because I love you and I need you to know that. I wish those early morning breakfasts were really so sweet smelling and warm, steaming bathtub beside the kitchen stove. I have to go grandma, to let go of my fear of your rejection and my fear that some of our family and community may reject me, deny my truth. I don't think this is such a great way to say good-bye but I guess it's not really good-bye because it's not over.

Love you,
Marcia

MOTHER IN THE NEWS
for Ann Weyaus

she is news: her right arm holds up
log big enough it broke the front window
she posed for the camera proud to tell
everyone in this part of town her rights
she won because she fought back fierce
a slum landlord, street punks, drunks

the fixed worry lines on her forehead
join two downward run grooves to lips
able to give a genuine grandma smootch

in the photo she has a short frizz perm
no stoic tranquil braids for her look
she don't play the instant elder role

her terrified girl story kept hidden
from the mother with a loaded gun
pointed at what now is a smiley face
she remembered that mother with tears
so we young ones would tell her forget
this misery mother needs to be told

get lost
not wanted back mother
unless you behave better
more like a mother

she stayed a scared woman years after

tobacco is a gift to give to elders
but she gave out smokes we craved
how generous this woman got
  since she told us her mother story

couple drags made my smoke cloud
under it I would also remember

Marie Annharte Baker

the next to last time I saw my mother

she was supposed to visit me
that time she got out of jail
the Mother's Day card I bought
with satiny feel floral teapot
I pressed the sponge padded spot
up and down milking the belly
teapot for a mother daughter touch

my mother kept me waiting
for affection time after time
but that time got cut off short
a bartender drowned out her asking
more beer if bootlegger how much

closing time move along lady
closing down beer parlor woman
closing me up to close up looks

I just for the fun of it dust off
her memory brush her bones
ever tickley
make her fancy laugh again & again

I set up archeology expeditions
but digging up mom takes work
news of where did she go abandon me
I turn instead to faded old newspaper
clipping to brag about this fighter mom

this mom is not in a skeleton closet
not checked out in the obits mother

but my birth mother I find stuck in
a heart-shaped pincushion she made
I talk straight to buried needles
she left memories in me deep hurts
stab my heart velvet soft and worn

FOUR DIRECTIONS AFTER HER LIFE
*Dedicated to a parting of spirit at Jocelyn House, Winnipeg

Extinct her animal

She survives a skeletal but not skeptical poem. I see her lioness kicked in the jaw, hunched down in a dry mud gully panting. Me, the big lens. Close up. She clicks her dose of pain killer. Shoot over. She waits for death and I give up Wild World of Animals obsession. Told she was dying. I came to look.

Mother our secrets

She again will escape bad poetry nights. She'll squint at the blur on what is left of a peeled beer bottle label. Mother words punctures her hang-over ear drums with tympany. Mothers we became. Imagination makes do for shot-up conversation with lies we told each other. Her booze mother confronted mine. All-Star Mother Wrestling except one died before treatment was invented. More mothers die for a planet. Exit the poison environment mother. Her shrine is waste. Wanted: a placebo poem mother. Plug in the dildo. Turn on the appliance mom, shiny chrome sides to hold toast, brew a cup, or spin dry, launder up generation shame blame.

Cant bear

Talk about bears on t.v. Polar bears declared a protected species. Why kill for a coat someone? Each animal I mention is almost extinct. No talk about her dying. We both barely know bears. And, bears know more about humping. Bears enjoy one another. Play around. Even the quickie takes more time for them. Quickest lover she ever had: answered a Personal ad, came at the door, introduced himself as he left. Missed out on the physical part. What if he just wanted a bear coat? Didn't want the bear. Her suffocation under the heat of polar bear skin on humid day. Her heat. Her hot. Her fur intact. Bears know how to die. Surrender hot gall bladders. For someone else to heal.

Marie Annharte Baker

Sweetgrass talks

Her Patsy Cline song made her walk after midnight. Sweetgrass talks. Makes walk same as talk. Whips around in the mind mother. Connects wild mouth organ back to the tongue. Should stick. Stay in place. Keep the tongue from prying open the coffin. Not out talked, let's hear one midnight singsong. That voice busy at last rites. Told off shake'n bake medicine man. She saw instant elder cult vulture inside his skin. Faked him out. Told his bogus ass to his face. Hey, pretty fake poem. At her funeral, I can't bear to read this poem I wrote for me not for her. Her poem rubbed off the beer bottle by sleight of hand. My poem robs a fur-bearing animal of dignity. Don't want to rub fur the wrong way. Keep between us mother talk. Daughter anger.

GHOST RIDER

I come home from school each day and I place my briefcase wherever it drops, walk over to Mr. Coffee, brew a pot, and sit down to do the *Gazette* crossword while I wait for Kate's school bus. Usually. But there are times when I come home here and stare out my kitchen window down to the ugly grey street below and I wonder what in hell am I doing here. What in hell went wrong and what in hell is this life all about? And I get scared. And I travel back, back to the prairie where I was born and all this living and learning business started.

I remember my childhood birthday parties out in the park-like backyard at home. "Ring around the rosy, pockets full of posies, husha, husha, we all fall down." Begonias, lilacs, miniature yellow tea roses edging the garden and the lush green lawn my father tended to, often on bended knees as if in communion. This was his church.

I remember the fist fight with the notorious Marlene "Easy" Wheeler, who had it coming, and boy, did she get it...right square in the neck. She ducked, I missed and after a lot of screaming and scratching and rolling around in the dirt we somehow managed to peel ourselves apart. Three years later I stood up for her at her wedding where she got so plastered that in the middle of her thank-you speech, she barfed all over herself and into her roast beef dinner. She hung herself that winter.

And then there was the time when I was about six years old and I cornered Billy Lemay between my father's tool shed and the garage and kissed him hard on the lips - which was a feat in itself as I had to hold him down at the same time; and because he had a bad cold, his face became slicker'n snot on a doorknob and he laughed so hard he farted, which evened up the score quite nicely, I thought. He's a criminal lawyer today. Successful, too, I hear.

I can smell the prairie air sometimes. I can feel the warm breeze on my face softly whispering sweet nothings in my ear. I'd stop my car in the middle of nowhere, get out and just look out in every direction as far as the eye could see over the golden sea of wheat.

Jeannine Peru

And if you're patient and a good listener, you can even hear the weather change. And then there's the meadow larks, my favourite of the winged people who sit up on the telephone wires, whistling their one-two one-two-three-four's at me, reminding me that this is indeed Eden. Skies of blue like a cathedral ceiling. Michelangelo couldn't paint this one: the prairie...home.

I'd get back into my car and drive on up the road, losing myself, burying myself in this living canvas, never ever wanting to be found. I'd imagine 'someone' up there, anyone, looking down and they'd see this little red dot of a car snaking along that long black strip of road right into an invisible door, a portal, that no one else could see except for me and the Painter. And He'd reach down and close it behind me. Home again.

I look around my apartment that's in its usual state of chaos. It seems to be saying, "It's time to go home." The half-done Peter Pan puzzle that Kate and I started last night lying on the coffee table, books of all shapes, sizes and colours stacked up in teetering piles on the floor and desk, unfinished manuscripts and stories burying my typewriter, a slutty-looking Barbie doll lying on the sofa staring up at me with that insidious grin, and an old birthday card on the phone table that reads, "Life begins at forty!" Lies. And I feel tired and my eyes well up with the tears that often escape me on the bus, and for sometimes very little reason, I think. I saunter off into the bathroom and stare into the mirror and the tired face looking back at me with the red pained eyes that they said used to be so full of hope. Crying and crying, sitting on the bathtub, head buried in both hands, I reach over and flush the toilet to muffle the sobs. And I leave again.

It was raining sheets; thunder and lightning crashed, lighting up the barn in the backyard, making it look smoky blue and eerie. My best friend Pat and I quickly pulled on our Wellingtons and rain jackets, grabbed the "12" that we've been working on, a few carrots from the gunney sack by the back door and made a mad dash out to the barn. The dogs who had taken cover from the downpour would suddenly appear out of nowhere and jump up at us, doing back flips and spins in mid-air, barking at us the whole time as they chased us out to the barn.

I pull open the huge barn door. The horses' whinny a welcome to us and we whinny back and feed them the carrots. They're used to this, Pat and I hanging around the barn during a storm drinking 'Club,' listening to us babble on and on about Melnyk and Warkentin, our two cowboys, our 'men in waiting' I used to call them: waiting for Godot. And they'd always say that they didn't know no guy named Godot.

We'd sit on the bales of hay and remark on the fresh smell the rain had brought, and the smell of horse shit and cow shit and the rich smell of oozing black mud. The birds in the rafters would fly around rearranging themselves in order to get a bird's eye view of these two fools, one-half Inuit and the other half-Cree, who were going to share their dreams with one another as they always did, their innermost wishes and fears, their fuck-ups and oh yes...the gossip. But before starting the gossip session we'd always preface it with, "Keep yer mouth shut eh?" and the other would reply, insulted, "Don't I always?" Then BANG-we were off gossiping and no one and nothing was spared or sacred to us for everyone got it.

Glug, glug, glug. "Tastes like more," and off we'd go into the rain to the vendor seven miles up the now-muddy black road, following the ruts all the way to the St. Anne's Hotel and we'd remark that St. Anne is the patron saint of losers and I said, "That's why we like the place so much and that's why we're going there now: like attracts like."

The people in the area used to call the four of us "outlaws," but the frustrated housewives used to love to call us whores and we'd laugh when we'd hear this for if they'd known us they'd have realized right quick that yes, we were a lot of things but whores wasn't one of 'em and anyway coming from them we didn't put much stock in it for we knew that deep down in their heart of hearts they'd rather be with us. But they didn't have what it takes; the balls to walk out on your life and we'd laugh even though we both knew that one day we'd pay. No one rides for free.

We'd leave the vendor after some friendly chitchat with the

owner, 'Snake Eyes,' as we called him behind his back, 'cause he'd always rape us with those beady black eyes of his each time we'd go in there. He was always trying to proposition us with the finesse of a Klik sandwich: "Why, howdy there, ladies. Why doncha come on up to my 'office,' (which was said to be a tiny room in the back with nothing but a smelly old cot in it) and we'll kill a "40" of Jack Daniels." And one day I said to him that I already had one asshole in my pants and I didn't need another one. We left with our case, Snake Eyes watching us through the window, hands in his pockets, no doubt, and we drove off into the storm, the lightning lighting up the road for us as we sang along to our favourite tape of the "Big O" at the very very top of our lungs, beer between our legs, deeper and deeper and farther and farther into the heart of the prairie. Two riders on the storm. Two dreamers, both never wanting to wake up, never wanting to take part in the real world. We'd both been bashed and mangled enough by it.

I often used to remind Pat that if this were the days of the Wild West that she and I would either be riding pintos out on this here prairie or we'd be long dead by now. I'd tell her that we'd be outcasts in the tribe 'cause the women would never go for the shit we were pulling: her cheating on her two-timing husband Dick, whom I once told after he had threatened me with a .22, that his mother must've been psychic to have chosen such an appropriate name for him, and me going out with a married guy. And Pat always loved to say at this point that for sure I'd be dead, hung out to dry by some Cree woman for taking her man. And then I'd remind her what the Cree used to do to cheating wives: cut off the tip of their noses and exile them to the lone prairie where nobody else would have anything to do with them...'cept maybe a dozen or so warriors from an enemy tribe who would find her out there. And she'd say that she could live with that as long as that's all they cut off. Cocky as hell we were. Heading for the wall. We took all the happiness we could and justified it by the hell our lives had been. We played hard. And we paid hard...just like we expected all along.

I thought of the guy I had met a few years back. It was the first time in a long time that I had let myself fall for someone again. He was a good guy, a great talker, funny as hell and just loved my Kate and she loved him. I could see a future with this guy and he saw one with us. And then one day after we'd been going out for about three months, he went to the emergency complaining of stomach pain and they opened him up, closed him up again and he died. Cancer. He was 38. Shee-it! And then one night I decided to ask for a dream. I wanted to see if he was OK. I wanted to say good-bye as I wasn't with him when he decided to "check out." I got the dream and he said to me, "Be careful," and he leaned over and ever so softly kissed me on the cheek. He turned to leave and I grabbed him by the leg, trying to pull him back, and then an old man dressed all in white and with a long white beard came forward and with his hand pulled open a portal and they both walked through it to disappear. I immediately woke up and whispered, "Good-bye." The wall.

Sometimes I feel as if I'm still there with Pat and Melnyk and Warkentin. We all keep in touch now and then and it's weird as hell 'cause all of us feel the same way about the past and one another, but we've all got our 'emergencies' on.

Warkentin, I hear, is losing one of the things he cherished most, his hair, and he's back with his wife again...playing house. And the news is that Betty Sky Hawk saw him just the other day in Super Valu pushing a grocery cart. Said she barely recognized him with that silly looking rug sitting way up there on that pointy little head of his. Said by the way he was winkin' and all...he's biting at the bit to play again.

Melnyk just got outta jail after four years inside, and is now starting over with his new old lady out on a farm on the Alberta/Montana border. They say he's punching cattle now instead of people. And each time I hear his voice, THAT voice that I once knew so well, I remember the day that he asked me to run away with him. I wonder where I'd be today if I'd said yes. But I didn't say yes and so he said that he'd take a rain check. It's pouring.

And Pat's still with Dick, waiting for the day she says that I pull into her yard. She wants to play again.

And me. Well I'm here physically but my spirit is there on the prairie. If I go back it'll start all over again, for Pat has often said that if I go back our cowboys will ride in and take us off and the four of us will all ride out together on this life that each one of us seems to be having such a damned hard time living. And we'll ride out on reality; A.W.O.L. And this is the reason that I've stayed here so long, too long. For if I go home...I'll never come back for I won't be able to. Jig's up. The wall.

Pat says I'm a ghost rider, a lone rider roaming the lone prairie, drifting and searching.

Sometimes when she's out riding in the fields she says she can feel me ride up beside her. And we ride for a spell.

Jacqueline Oker

WAITING FOR THE WELFARE CHECK

Your Honour
I didn't ask to be brought before you
I took the milk from the shelf to feed my new born
She is only a month old
My welfare check didn't come in
I had to do this

My breasts have become contaminated with poisons
from the land that was once pure
They have become ice cold
The milk has become dark brown
It no longer tastes sweet
My child can't take my sickness
and be expected to survive

Your Honour
I grew up on welfare
I know what it's like to be hungry
You look in the cupboard and it's empty
Stomach aching
Tears fall
Mother gone to find money
and not coming home until dawn
The little bit of food she brings
is gone after a meal

Each agonizing day passes
Hopelessness sets in
School no longer important
I dropped out
Alone with no guidance
I followed the footsteps of my mother
on welfare with a child
Surviving anyway I could
to feed a hungry mouth
from month to month

Jacqueline Oker

Your Honour
My baby's father he wants nothing to do
with us because he's
in the Kingston Pen for life
I'm left to raise my child on my own
I live in a run-down one-bedroom apartment
The floor squeaks with each step
Water constantly drips from taps
The walls yellow with age
hole marks all over
the rug stained with cigarette burns
Mice run around at night
scaring me and my baby
For this place I pay $400.00 per month

Welfare gives me only $500.00
I have left only a hundred dollars
to buy groceries for me and my child
Because we are now out of food
I have not eaten since yesterday
Why don't I move? you ask yourself
I can't because the welfare department
will not pay out more for me to live better

Your Honour
I'm a Indian women
They treat us all the same
They believe because we have brown skins we are tough
We are human beings with feelings
Me and my Indian sister
we are no better or worse than your neighbour
Does he not have
a desire to make a better life for his family?

Your Honour
If I knew my native tongue
I could return to the rez
and get a job
It's not my fault

Jacqueline Oker

I was never taught
my language
It's also not my fault
my father abandoned me
I never knew his name
Never saw a picture
I was just another
Indian bastard born to a squaw

Your Honour
It's not my choice
I have ended up this way
at 21 years old
When I close my eyes
I have dreams
of becoming a successful doctor
working in a clean hospital
I work my 12 hour shift and I go home
to a home-cooked meal
and to a man who loves and respects me
I'm balanced, stable, and happy
I see myself get off this merry- go- round
But when I open my eyes
and hear my baby's hungry cries
I realize it's only a dream
Something that can happen
to those white women
but not to this brown-skinned squaw

Your Honour
because I grew up this way
I never learned my culture
I never seen a pow-wow
nor a drum
I haven't been able to
get to the Friendship Centre
to meet my fellow Indians
I have no money to get across town
I'm stranded here

Jacqueline Oker

---

making my way to the Salvation Army
soup line-ups
when the hunger is too much
Each day passes
as my child and I wait with empty stomachs
for that check to come in

Your Honour
The clothes on my back are all I own
I can't afford to buy anything
I have been going to the Salvation Army's
free store
to pick up clothes for my growing baby
They say I can only make
two more visits before
I have my limit of clothes
What am I to do?
Each night I worry for her
I wonder how I am going to make ends meet
from month to month
I want her to have a better life
to be stronger than me
so she can get out of this cycle

Your Honour
I have no pictures of my baby
If you put me behind bars
The welfare department
will for sure
take her and put her in a foster home
I will only remember her
innocent smile through my memory
They will not return her to me
because I'm on welfare
and I stole for her survival

Your Honour
I beg you please let me walk away free today
I don't have money to pay a fine

Jacqueline Oker

I can't do community service work
because I have no babysitter for my child
If I leave her those welfare people
will be at my door
ready to snatch her from my arms

Your Honour
I did what
I did only because of my baby
As you sentence me
Think about what I have said to you
today
My story is no different
than other cases you've heard
I want no pity from you
just some understanding
as to why I had to take the milk from
the store shelf

Your Honour
I can't guarantee
that you won't see me again
next month
for stealing milk
or the month after that
for stealing baby pabulum
I'm caught in a terrible cycle
that can't be helped
as I wait for my welfare check
to come in

Your Honour
Is trying to survive
such a crime?

This is all I have to say.
Thank-you, Sir

Colin T. Jarrett

WHO'S THE MONSTER - A Song

The Gum tree cries
    Alone
His world is shattered.

He hears,
    the noise of Destruction.
And sees,
    the Monster
    heading his way.

The Monster has destroyed
his family and friends.
Their bodies lie everywhere.

Only yesterday
    they all lived in Peace.
As they have for Eons.

Their inhabitants were all happy-
The bees making honey
and birds singing in their nests.
Lizards sunbaking on their limbs,
ants busily scurrying around their trunks.

    Then came the Monster.

Some of the birds dive at
    the Destroyer.
While others try to distract it.

Bees try to sting it,
Lizards try to bite it,
the winds blow harder.
But nothing can stop the Monster.

Colin T. Jarrett

The Gum tree, by now
has accepted his Fate.
His tragedy is shared by all.

He feels the teeth
of the Monster,
around his trunk.

He cries
in the agony of Death,
as he feels his roots
     being cruelly torn
     from the Earth.

     He sees the ground,
     rushing towards him.

The Gum Tree lies alone-
     Dying.

NIGHTMARE

Like a hungry panther along the lake ridge at Oconoluftee, he is following every breath and every movement I make. I can feel the weight of his eyes pushing down on my shoulders, pinning me, forcing me up against the rocks and the violence begins, like an urban riot unleashed on one small woman.

The initial blow knocks the force of life from me and I am defenseless–like jell-o. My head is like a punching bag suspended in a gym. The battery of blows continues until I can't feel my face anymore, then the jabs and punches land in my ribs. The blood running out my ears and nose is almost soothing.

I hear his voice somewhere in the distance and jerk myself awake by myoclonic spasm; my dad taught me to wake myself up from nightmares this way when I was about three or four years old. Remember, the dreams you're falling in and you land and wake at the same time and the bed is shaking? It's like that. When I wake I am soaked with sweat; goosebumps form rows all over my skin. I make myself move, turning to sit up. The quivering slows, my teeth stop chattering and I breathe in deeply, rhythmically. I get up and walk around the house checking locks and latches on doors and windows, then I splash some cool water on my face to snap me out of the dream.

My kids are crying, afraid of me screaming in my sleep. They've been up for hours, as usual, but it's so hard for me to sleep at night I wait for light to come to rest easier, sometimes. Usually, by the time I do, I'm caught in nightmares until I force myself awake. Poor things, probably hungry, too. Always my ex – my kid's dad. That is the worst feeling when one of your own people tries to kill you on a daily basis; my own tribe, one of my own people, he even has more blood than me – almost full.

Twelve years ago he was a very good-looking man. Long, dark hair and dark brown eyes — haunting. No one told me he was on parole, or that he beats women. I knew he drank, but I was just a young kid then and I drank my share, too. No one said he was sick and cruel. As a man he came to me in disguise — all smiles, all laughter. All of the girls wanted him, and he wanted me. When the laughter went away, the maniac emerged. The man was vicious, psychopathic.

It has been behind me for a long time — nine years — and that much time has passed since I laid eyes on him. He said he would never bother me again, but he lives on still, inside this realm of sleep in my mind. Every time I think I might try life again, he comes in dreams – haunting me. Every time I think I am over my past, something triggers him and calls him back.

I tried to visit my family last winter. They were living in a one-bedroom trailer house. We used to have one just like it when we were married. I was trying to visit with my dad and I felt like I was in a tin coffin. I flashed back to lying on the floor, face down, with a five-month old baby under me to protect him from flying bullets. That tiny infant and his dad at war with somebody, probably a neighbour, maybe a stranger. I got claustrophobic and paced all night. I drove my family nuts jumping out of bed and running through the trailer looking out windows throughout the night, not completely conscious — on automatic pilot — half asleep, still dreaming.

I have been in severe depression for twelve weeks this time, no explanation. I think about a man I was with who really cared for me and left here...I want to be over there with him...I feel incredibly tired. There is much sadness around us all the time, the beauty is lost in it, over there it is good.

I relive the guns held on me and knives, the beatings, the wrecks, the broken bones and spirit, the ruptured organs — all night sometimes. I don't want to lie down to face it again.

My dad is a World War II vet. He tells me that the Indians were all scouts or radio men over there; he was both. The Philippines, Solomons, New Guinea – the army never gave him any of the medals or decorations he won. I have seen the discharge papers with the awards list. He said that they just stuck him on a bus to the nearest town and cut him loose. I wrote to the V.A. in 1989. He finally got six of the medals and some of the ribbons in 1990 — almost fifty years late.

He looks at me like he is going through me. He says he knows what bothers me in the night. He knew it himself after he came back from the war. He says hand-to-hand jungle warfare were the best and worst days of his life. The best because he felt the warrior in him (a part of our society that has been taken away leaving the men feeling that they lack something they often try to replace in military service), the worst because of the death and destruction of life.

He tells me when you live through severe violence on a day-in, day-out basis — when you are held hostage — trying to survive each hour of each day, the violence can come back again, over and over. He tells me the Vietnam vets are calling it post-traumatic stress syndrome, today. He says war is war, no matter which home front it takes place on. He tells me to recognize it and to pray about it — to face it and face the dream.

I turn on KILI Radio — Lakota airwaves, 100,000 watts strong and I listen to the D.J. talk with a white doctor from Pine Ridge, IHS, about the Indian suicide rate and its rise in the winter, how it increases with the cold. I wonder how many people relive their days of terror, how many pasts haunt today. How many vets, how many abused women and children, all lying awake at night.

I open a can of commode meat and fix my kids some lunch.

her

I have seen her as i sit in this bar in Toronto
she is in the corner
dark hair
beaded earrings
black eyes
that see through me
she has power she has strength I reach for her
she is gone

She fades by the time I've had my 4th beer
by the time i have had my 5th she is gone
replaced
by anyone else i see
blonde hair diamond earrings unseeing eyes
there is no power
she is gone

I have seen her on the street
driving by i called out to her
the wind took away my voice
and scattered it
across the prairies into the bush lost in the sunset

Trying to sweat
cleanse the poison
see her with sober eyes
she has power she has strength I reach for her
she will be waiting for me
only when i am ready

Beyond the Convent Door

"Ke chi Okimaw, he is the King who lives beyond this door and this place is his place." Thus we whisper, children of a lesser order and we savor our heathen noises, "Mah. (Listen)" and for a few minutes no nun comes and only the wavering light beneath the nuns' chapel door moves and later, between the nuns' patrolling footsteps, we lie in our stiff beds, talking quietly about Okimaw and how is it, someone says, that he gave out baskets of bread to the hungry people...when here in his own house he locks it up..."Yes, I saw it too-chains, big ones, and a padlock too. Yes, I do not think he is the real one," and the night's quiet is punctuated with the belly-rumbling of one collective agreement. "Too, he makes us get up early and never even comes, not even when Sister Teresa hit that new girl right on her head with that big steel brush." So we speak sometimes when it is quiet. Then we hear someone crying - probably because they've wet the bed - and won't the nuns like this in the morning but we, the eight and nine-year olds, know that it's always this way for the new ones. "Don't cry," we say. "When you get big like us you won't be doing that or crying anymore." But we lie. Sometimes, when it is almost morning and I've been thinking of God for some time, I cry slowly so no one will hear me and I think it doesn't matter because Okimaw, he doesn't really live here.

They Still Talk
(For Anna Mae Pictou Aquash)

I have had many hands touch me
My grandfather's at death looked like clay

and when I rounded a corner in Penticton BC
a man lay on the sidewalk
less one thing he needed
and his hands looked like clay too

and the night before last

I picked up a dream in the middle of the night
but when I rolled the body over
fingers dug into my eyes

Anna Mae
Anna Mae...Anna Mae

I tried to hold onto the image of your severed hands
I see now they held the cry of your people

I cried the day I was told

and every winter day
I wake to the smell of kerosene
the memory of agents camping out

and the pair of boots
that led them to you

your hands
in this life time
had many things to say

they touched
lovers
molded children
held brothers and sisters

and you and me

and they still talk...

Chief Shining Armour

Her eyes frantic
search longingly beneath
the deep black pools
of her sundance snag

His wrinkles fresh
dry of wisdom
illuminate
the truth she uncovers there

a painful reality
woven
hidden amongst the
tantalizing illusion
of a warrior archetype

frozen in fantasy
she savours...

His long black braids   Lies
    slither between   Ridicule
        dark defined nipples   Drunk
            buckskin molds   Abuse
                his masculine muscles
                    tall and proud
                        he stands to protect her
                  His studly sunglasses
                ride the end of his long straight nose
        full round lips
        caress her with pretty words of honour
            he respects her woman power   Rape
        bows to her moontime   Exclude
    Medicine Man   Oppress

Chief Shining Armour
she pleads to him to stay
as he fades back into the
large black pools
of her sundance snag

But her words lost
echo back to her
from across a distending canyon.

duncan mercredi

Esquaw

woman   standing in shadows
caught in the glare of headlights
eyes downcast
stepping into the path of pain
rising from your past
covered in residential clothes
blending into the word of god
spoken unspoken mute
whipped into shape by fear
your power drained by ignorance and lies

oh woman   in shadows
weep in silence
watching your child forced from you
not from your demons
but from those who carry their pipes
using them as weapons
much like the sign of the cross

oh   woman   shadows
covered caskets haunt you
weep at each little breath
torn from within you
let the salt from your tears
brown the land
oh   woman   weep

HOW MUCH LONGER

Sitting.
Sane on the outside
going bloody crazy
alone in my mind.
The denial, it speaks so softly
gently weaves a comforting lie
whisper, whisper again
keep my child safe in there.

Will it be much longer?

I don't feel like going on.
Place your hands on my chest
feel my breastbone.
Imagine the pain;
a knife going in;
the shock of a bullet exploding
through soft flesh and bone.

Is it going to be much longer?

It's the pain. I try to stop it
I talk. The men and women
they ask, "Do you always feel like this?;
Is this a normal way for you to feel?"
I feel good, then I feel so tired.
They say, "You have survived, you are strong."

Will it ever be over?

Debby Keeper

All the energy
the effort to conceal
within a mask the pain
that eats my soul,
destroys my mind.
Its release burns my eyes
and I can't see
that Beauty and Love
once had a place
for me.
Only when it rains
am I real
when the tears
can't be seen
when I'm not forced to smile
(and be here).

How much longer?

Lemon Tea Reminds Me Of Encampments And Velaciones

Lemon grass tea
sweetened
welcomes me
on nights of winter encampments
or long velaciones holding warmth
Little sister lemon grass
Older sister
    in the cycle
    gives me strength
    to carry on
Aroma
breath
life
    sensations
    penetrating

Standing by the sacred fire
working through exhaustion
community granting feeling
ceremonial unity
in place of
stressful fragmentation

Being warmed from hands
to toes to nose
and all throughout inside
with love
as even now
in this cold encampment
of my room
at this velorio for my self

Ines Hernandez-Avila

I break the fever
toxins released in sweat
like tears
with her warmth
      honeyed
      healing
      of my soul
and my spirit
alerted
takes careful steps
of recovery
back
to me

Northern Wind Song

Grandmother
I hear your wind song
enchant
drums echo
awakening ghost dancers
whose shadows
brush the red willow
mist forms
Dene-Deh
rise to your wind song
northern wind song
keeper
of the people

Grandmother
I lay my heart on the land
carry me home
beyond snow-blown dreams
to the tea dance
round fires dance round fires
with my ancestors
round fires dance round fires
to the beat of your
northern wind song
we become
keepers
of the land

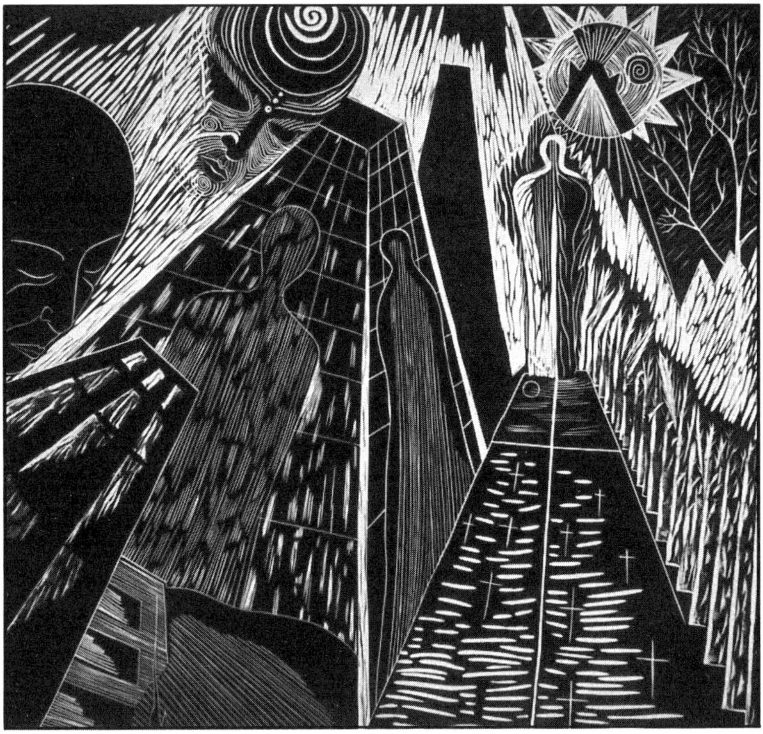

Fire

Jane Inyallie

FIRE

i drift
on a plane
of
sleep

your whisper
lures me
into
veils of silver

entwined
we
slide
the
spiral valley

we
spin
cry out
call
A'tsoo
keeper
of
eternal
fire

she draws us
to her potency
we suckle
burning breasts
flesh and bone
melt away

flames
writhe
red
dancing
the sacred
womb
of
ecstasy

Gloria Roberds

REFLECTIONS OF YOUR GLORY DAYS

Memories unwind
pausing my stride
as I see you
meander the streets.
Gestures and mumbles
enforce the depths
of your dis-orientation.
Passers-by react differently.
Some recoil with disgust,
others pause compassionate.
Very few remember your past.
The ones who do,
give you something
cash or smokes
sometimes both.
Bulkiness announces bundled clothes
layered for insulation
against cold or heat.
You look seventy
instead of forty.

Our first meeting,
where the Trans-Canada
flows under the bypass bridge
just past Banff's turnoff,
I, seated on a rock,
nibbled at a light snack
slowly swallowed a tepid Coke
You and your friend,
fresh from Manitoba,
looking for work -
bound for Vancouver.
Like a tennis-player spectator
my head swung
one side to the other.
due to your argument:
DO or DON'T pick up the Indian

Gloria Roberds

---

so obviously pregnant.
You won.
We spent fourteen years committed.
Your declaration of
"the need and will to be a family man.
The unborn would be as your own"
created a change of
You and me
The roles slipped on so comfortable.

The abandonment of responsibilities
other than food and a bed -
A totally new concept for me.
Hitch-hiking on Indian time
pausing for a day's work,
then moving on
Money in the pocket.
Two as one
against the world.

The tips of your fingers and thumbs
calloused from shingler's work;
fantastic finger strength
used quarters to flip off pop caps.
An intense tea drinker
Talking eyes behind such long lashes.
You sure had mixed feelings
cause your Mom had given you the boot
right after burying your Dad.
Didn't want no grown boys about
While she talon-held a boyfriend
to be a prospective husband.

You always gave the shirt off your back,
a fierce fighter for the underdog.
The inseparable twins
compassion and consideration
were the heart of your daily life.
Never lost in idleness
always doing something.

Gloria Roberds

The most silver warped board
made into creative art -
creations of beauty and usefulness.
The laughter you produced
when you'd test-proof your work.
Does one forget a 180 pound man
dancing on a child's table?
Tin-rusted, warped and mangled
straightened and polished
lovingly shaped and moulded
toys, furnishings, knickknacks.
Leatherwork lived and breathed
under your touch
"Jack of all trades,"
You could fix anything
wiring, autos, childish woes.

At the Vedder Crossing Motel,
upon returning to pay rent
we were met by eight determined men
bent on gaining our welfare cheque.
You stood your ground.
Clenched your teeth.
Your eyes had already picked the ringleader.
Ordering me behind you,
(Me-eight months pregnant)
You told me to find you a club.
Sent me to phone the cops.
Then demanded I wait at the cafe
until your arrival.

Darren at three-months-old
truly deflated
your ego
all because we thought it was too cold
to take our daily walk after supper.
How his eyes were drawn
to sparkling jewels,
flashing traffic lights.
His complete attention captivated

Gloria Roberds

by anything that moved or made a sound.
His angry screams raged throughout the hotel
till we dressed him and donned his woollen cap.
For three days
he turned his head from you and
stilled his gurgling chatter
That penance tortured you indelibly.

Residing at the Sunora Hotel
you picked apples;
You had never ever done it before.
The straps created blisters
two inches high on your shoulders.
I sat you in the sun -
poured on Johnson's baby lotion.
Each time the sun's heat
penetrated it into your skin
I'd reapply it.
You tolerated my actions.

Early the next morning
Ol' Frank was amazed-
you hale and hearty,
ready for work.
He couldn't believe you were blister free.
He asked you the remedy,
you winked and said
"Old Indian medicine. Ask her."

The Sunora room,
like a cellar pantry
all walls, no windows
only one door to enter.
You had just left,
gone to the Valley
for a couple of drinks.
A late fall storm
blew out the town's power.
Everything was impenetrable black
I grabbed the baby and

backed against the wall.

Eyes locked on the unseen entrance
voices...sounds intensified
swelling fears battled logic
my heart threatened to rupture,
burst through my rib cage.
My mind locked, concentrated
"Breathe normal"
my brain screamed
"Black be my friend;
Black be their enemy."

"She's home alone. He's gone."
"Are you sure?"
"I seen him leave."
"I don't know."
"It's black, nobody will recognize us
Come on! We're safe."
"They'll hear us."
"They won't see us."

The two men's footsteps
cautiously approached the door.
But behind them
heavy steps rustled
with forward determination.
A voice commanded
"Hey! You two! Stop!"
A candle sputtered...quavered for life.
Across the hall to the left
its light flickered towards the door
but fell short
revealed Ol' Frank's shadowy presence.
He grabbed two men,
knocked their heads together,
and tossed them toward the descending stairwell.

As Ol' Frank demanded a chair and candle,
placing his bulky frame dead centre of the doorway,

Gloria Roberds

---

your protective panic slammed the front door shut.
Haste bounced your body off the walls
in your ascent to me.

At the stairtop you leaped over
the fetal cowards,
and made a mad sprint into our room.
Still feeling desperate,
I clasped you to me
drawing so much energy from you
I almost smothered the babe.
Your intuitive radar
always placed you near
in times of dire need.
Marian Elizabeth named for your sisters
holds a certain spot in your heart
because she's the first-born that you've raised
which was a bonus for family members
to use as a lever to attend family-do's.
I remember if we wanted to go somewhere,
if each one of us asked, you said "no."
But you could never say no to Marian.
How your eyes shone...flamed!
Mingled emotions of frustration, pride, love
the battle of wanting to say no but couldn't
radiated from your body at my underhandedness.

Frederick William named after our fathers
exploded into an early birth
due to a shower suddenly turned cold.
Three pounds four ounces.
If he made it over forty-eight hours he'd live.
Vivid are the agonizing hours of praying,
willing strength into that minuscule life.
Tubes were plugged into his mouth
navel, nostrils and behind his ankles.
Little patches stuck to his head and chest.
All our senses screeched-he's a hair from death.
Your parental instincts were strong.
You'd put your hands into the incubator cubby holes

talk to him, lift him and stroke him with your finger.
I was petrified of holding him in case I broke him.
He was so soft and warm.
Like a piece of sponge covered with velvet,
his little body was half the width of your palm.
You only needed one finger to hold his head.
His little kinked legs touched the top of your wrist.
I never held him until he was two and a half months.

Robin Laura, our English Rose,
named for you and my Mother.
The first time I went into labour
they induced me to reverse the contractions.
The second time they wanted to do the same.
I demanded to deliver now
or I'd catch the next bus to Penticton.
Three days after her birth,
the doctors said it was crucial to operate.
If her skull wasn't opened
it would grow deformed and her brain wouldn't grow.
It's a miracle she never drowned.
All those tears we shed.
Stricken with horror and terror we debated.
Finally I signed the paper for the go-ahead.
She was such a happy smiling baby.
Her eyes would sparkle alive with her emotions.
She is still a dreamer.

The day at Kingsway and Broadway
we were headed to Safeway
(you and "Sissi" being regular chatterboxes).
Suddenly I saw an elderly lady fall
about three steps off the curb into a crossing;
noon hour traffic just a whistling by.
She lay belly down in the street
raised the length of her arms,
paling with each whizzing vehicle.
Fear-locked words couldn't mobilize my ironed muscles.
My eyes bulged as my mind willed her to rise.
My unguided hand finally clutched your shirt sleeve;

Gloria Roberds

turning, you followed my gaze.
Towards the fallen lady you flew
in the process you grabbed a "four x four x ten"
Stepping in front of the fallen one,
you stood with the raised board
like a titan gladiator, defiant and brazen,
Ready to take one and all through death's gate.
Drivers whitened and swerved around you.
A little red sports car came, turned and
blocked traffic securely in the double lane.
The driver, a young man, jumped out to assist you.
The poor woman had elephantiasis,
couldn't bend her knees or ankles.
Together you raised and aided her to the curb.
We, the family, waited at the bus bench.
You slowly walked her home
and carried her things while she talked,
made a pot of tea and waited till her colour returned.

Christopher John, our last babe.
2 A.M. Born New Year's Day.
A howling blizzard raged.
It was a tight situation to get a sitter.
Everyone was off to a New Year's Eve party somewhere.
I told you not to come until you found a sitter.
So between each breath you had to run home.
You'd open the door, gasping for breath,
and stand in the doorway,
leaning the left arm on the door frame,
the right clasping the doorknob;
breathless, you'd quickly babble
as wind and snowflakes danced chaotic
past your perspiring body.
No wonder Chris is the calmest during the wildest storms.
No wonder he's such an action person.
Chris, our own stormwalker.

Society laced and braided your downfall.
Certified and papered carpenters came to you
inquired, received and used your knowledge

learned from your father and grandfather
yet ironically refused you full-time jobs.
Social workers continually agitated.
It pinched your esteem.
Your future dreams shrivelled and died.
There was so much support to drink and forget your troubles.
Finally you admitted defeat and
signed everything over to me,
released me and the children,
you decided to play the game they called alcoholism
and released yourself totally.
Now...you're a wino...on the street.
Will it only be a passing phase?
Please don't let it be until death do you part.
Shared hardships and good times
created a special place in our hearts
that can never be taken away or replaced.
The offsprings asked if I'd ever take you back.
Oftentimes I replied there's too much water under the bridge,
only God can see and predict the future.

Bernelda Wheeler

REFLECTIONS IN A BUS DEPOT

One of her most treasured memories as a young mother was the time when her girl was six. A little four-year old boy lived next door and he was forbidden to go into the basement in his house. His dad had a lot of fine tools, some of them dangerous, so that boy was told to stay out of the basement.

Well, another older little boy lived in the same neighbourhood. This boy was pampered and spoiled...did almost anything he wanted to do without having to account for his actions. He seemed to be obsessed with the desire to go into that basement. One day he hounded that little four-year old until finally they both went to the basement. The mother caught them, and oh, that poor little four-year old got a terrible scolding. Not only that, his mother said as soon as his dad got home she was going to tell on him and he would get punished, for sure.

Notokwesiw's girl saw and heard all this and went running home in a panic. Almost in tears she told her mom what happened. "And Jamie's going to get a good licking and it's not even his fault," she said.

"So what do you think we should do then?" Notokwesiw asked her girl.

"I have to tell his dad what happened because I tried to tell his mom and she wouldn't listen to me. It wasn't Jamie's fault, that other boy made him go into the basement."

Notokwesiw looked at her girl. "What time does this dad come home my girl?"

"I don't know, but I have to wait for him and I have to tell him the truth for Jamie. Jamie's mom won't listen to us."
"Go on then, but if you need anything you call me."

Whimpering and half running, Notokwesiw's girl went next door and sat on the door step. All afternoon that girl sat there, waiting for the little boy's dad to come home. Once she had to call her mom because she had to go to the bathroom. Notokwesiw had to stand outside in case that dad came home to explain to him that her girl had to tell him something before he went into the house. But it was allright; he didn't come home just then. Her girl went back and sat on the doorstep until that man got home.

Finally he was home. Notokwesiw's girl told him everything and saved that little boy from a punishment that he didn't deserve. Notokwesiw was so proud of her girl. She must have told that little story hundreds of times. Now her grandchildren knew the story. She was going to keep on telling that story too. Imagine that, she thought to herself; my girl was only six and already she was fair and honest. That girl was now in her thirties and had a daughter of her own. She was still fair and honest.

Things seem to have settled down in the bus depot. The little girl was sleeping now, slumped down in one of those hard plastic chairs. Must be close to supper time, Old Woman thought. She was hungry by now. Good thing she had packed those fry bread and moose-meat sandwiches. Let's see now, she thought, where did I pack them? Oh yes, in that white plastic grocery bag. Now, where in the world did she put the white plastic grocery bag? Oh yes, in the little brown suitcase.

Old Woman remembered the two Roman Catholic brothers. Trying to set up a new order, those two called themselves Brothers of the Precious Blood or some damn thing like that. They ran a foster home for boys, but the boys they had were all disabled somehow. One of them had a bad heart and two of them were very, very slow learners. One of their boys later came to live at Old Woman's home. He was an orphan and had no place to live.

Well, those two Roman Catholic brothers were evil. They would get those boys drunk; then the one called brother Gerald would rape them. Her boy never really came right out and said it, but Notokwesiw believed those boys were put out for prostitution too. And then they were threatened that if they ever told, the brothers would have to tell on them too. Those poor boys got to believe that it was their fault

Bernelda Wheeler

---

what was happening and they were scared to say anything.

It took a long, long time, but through Notokwesiw's boy, and Notokwesiw's support, the case went to court. Three times the crown lawyer was changed and so many times Notokwesiw's poor boy almost gave up.

That brother Gerald used to watch him and Notokwesiw from his car. He'd follow them. He'd park his car in front of their house and just sit there. He threatened Notokwesiw's boy. Notokwesiw and her boy sometimes lived in terror. Months and months it was like that. They were scared to go out. They were scared to come home. But if they gave up, those church people would be free to brutalize other boys. They had to see it through. No matter how hard it was, they couldn't give up. And it was hard. How many times had Old Woman talked her boy into seeing it through when he was ready to quit. They would talk and discuss it for hours. Always they came to the same conclusion. They didn't want any more boys to have to suffer those indignities, that shame, that fear.

Somehow, they got through those long hard months. The time in court seemed so long. Notokwesiw phoned as many friends as she could think of, and invited them to sit in the courtroom while the trial went on. One of those brothers went to prison for that, but he only got three years. She didn't know how much time he spent in prison, but last Notokwesiw heard, he was trucking all over the north, preaching around again. Was that the way God's workers were supposed to conduct themselves?

Sad memories. Sad, sad memories.

But there were good memories too. Some of her boys came from reserves. One of them was a big strong young man. He wore glasses and everybody liked him. His name was James and he found lots of things to laugh about. The others used to try and make him laugh because he sounded so funny, like he had the hiccups or something. He was such a happy guy, that James. Seemed like he sparkled.

Oh yeah, then there was Cecil. Stubborn Cecil. Old One had taught all her boys how to cook and look after themselves, but Cecil was kind of lazy. Always watching TV with his finger buried in his mouth. Used to be scared of some TV shows; that boy wrapped himself in a blanket and covered his head when scary parts came on.

One time it was Cecil's turn to cook supper. All they ate that night was boiled potatoes and macaroni. Cecil didn't want Notokwesiw to tell him what to do, so he made supper the way he wanted it.

Another time Cecil got stubborn and refused to cook. All evening the boys sat around and went hungry. Then Cecil got hungry enough and he went in the kitchen to make himself a sandwich but the other boys wouldn't let him. "We want a decent supper", they said. And they kept trying to get Cecil to cook. He just sat and watched TV and tried to ignore them. But when the big Mac came on and he heard their stomachs grumbling Cecil had had enough. "Okay, okay, okay." he said. "I'll make your fuckin' supper."

It was a hungry bunch of boys that ate a late supper that night, but it was the last time Cecil got stubborn about cooking. Most of the time he was kind and gentle, and he felt guilty when he remembered how pitifully hungry they looked just because he was too lazy to cook. Even worse, their stomachs growled at him.

Ah, there were lots of memories of those years. Most of her foster sons came from away up north, all Cree speakers and they talked to one another in Cree most of the time. Old Woman only knew a little bit. They used to go car riding a lot and one time Notokwesiw told them a story that she thought was funny. When she finished her story there was no reaction but one of the boys was bright and intelligent and in Cree he scolded his brother and cousin, "It's a joke" he said in Cree, and he told them to laugh. So they all laughed hard, never mind that they didn't know what they were supposed to be laughing at. They had to be respectful and co-operative, they thought, even if that meant laughing at bad jokes they didn't understand.

Although there was nothing wrong with their intelligence or capa-

Bernelda Wheeler

bilities, they weren't all that good at English and sometimes used the language inappropriately. One of them brought a sock to Old Woman one time and asked her if she could fix it. "It's broken," he said.

They were quite thoughtful and protective of Old Woman too. They knew she didn't like fighting so they wouldn't tell her about the fights they had or had witnessed. Years later, she learned that one time two of her boys had a hell of a fight, but they hid their bruises. Stole her make-up and every day they carefully put on the make up. What was their fight about? One of them told her, "We fighted over a nickel."

Kind of funny how those boys used to get back at her, too. One of them was mad at her for a long time. He was in art classes at school and one day he brought a gift home for Old Woman; it was a piece of clay work he did in pottery class, very well done piece of work, too. It was a closed hand with the middle finger sticking straight up in the air. She always knew when one of them was not happy with her; when it was his turn for cooking, he cooked all the things she didn't like. Another one didn't do or say anything, just gave her dirty looks at every opportunity.

Old Woman wanted her foster sons to be strong and independent, so she made sure they all made decisions together. They had to do as much around the house as Notokwesiw did, so they all learned how to cook and keep house. One of them even learned how to knit and another one could sew and crochet. When the Indian Affairs counsellor needed a home for a new boy, everybody got together and decided whether the new boy would move in or not.

Notokwesiw had loved her foster boys. Even when they were rotten little turds she loved them. She remembered those two boys who were always sleeping in. She couldn't get them up in the mornings. At last she talked with their school counsellor, and didn't he come right to the house...went right up to their room and got them out of bed for school. It was kind of amusing to see those two sleepy-headed boys coming down the stairs with bewildered looks on their faces. They kept looking at each other; didn't quite know what to think.

They didn't sleep in too often after that.

Notokwesiw snuck a look at the little girl. Poor little girl. Maybe....maybe some day something good would happen for her. Old Woman would pray hard for all the little kids who were scared.

Well, soon time for the bus. It was good to sit and remember sometimes. Now that she was getting old, Notokwesiw had time for herself and she often sat alone with her memories. Good memories, sad memories, funny memories, inspiring memories and painful, hurting memories, too. She'd often thought that if she could write, she would write stories about her special memories. There were so many of them.

Notokwesiw had to go to Thompson. Her girl was going away to school for a week, and Notokwesiw was going to look after her grandchildren. That was her job now. Look after grandchildren. It was a good job.

When she thought of little ones, she always remembered something a white doctor told her. Somebody wrote it she thought, something about...'children are our most valuable natural resource. They're non-renewable and they deserve the very best we can give them.'

It was a good way to think about the little ones.

The young mother and her little girl boarded their bus. That young mother still looked as though she was scared of something. It wasn't until their bus began to move that the mother relaxed. It looked as though she breathed a sigh of relief. She closed her eyes briefly, and then she looked at her little girl and smiled. Her girl smiled back and crawled onto her mother's lap. The last Notokwesiw saw of them they had their arms around one another. Their eyes were closed and they were both smiling. Notokwesiw smiled, too, as that bus took them to safety. Strange thing she thought, that bus is a safe place for those two.

Oh...there was her bus. Good places sometimes, these bus depots. Mind you, they could at least provide chairs that were comfortable.

Leona Hammerton

Silent Faces

Sometimes
late late at night
when loneliness crowds in
envelops
and enshrouds me with darkness
I breath in
the sacred sweet grass
and tears of sorrow
of empty waste
are recreated
into tears of joy
shared happiness
because then
when the smudge is done
the lingering aroma
still sweetens the air
my silent people
from silent memories
become reality

there are no words

for I have lost my language
silent faces
of gentle people
welcome me into their midst
and I know
that I am home
and I know
that my imagination
could never create this happiness
somewhere
from long long ago
I relive
precious memories

Pauline M. Mattess

Discovering me

I am a lot of things to different people.
I am my mother's child, my son's mother
my husband's wife.
I being all these other roles,
I lose myself.
I like who I am now, and the person
I am becoming is going to be even better.

Maxine Baptiste

DEFINITIONS

What is woman?	b e a u t y
female?	g r a c e
the fairer sex?	f o r m
	l o o k s
Who defines beauty?	a r e
delineates aestheticism?	f o u n d
	i n
Through whose eyes is beauty seen?	t h e
Through whose brain squeeze patterns	s p i r i t
of refinement?	i n
of splendor?	t h e
	mind
subliminal messages	i n
of symmetrical form	t h e
take shape	w o r d s
	i n
picture perfect preconceived ideas	t h e
materialize	t h o u g h t s
manifest a predestination of appearance	i n
	t h e
disallowing any other aspect	memory
	i n
imperceptible turns to distinction	t h e
	s m i l e s
silhouettes of shadows assume semblance	i n
march across dimly lit corridors of a mind befuddled with	T
caricatures of character characterizations	H
categorize female counterparts into cubby holes	E
cartooning collapsible creatures	
columnizing already fragile dispositions	
into comfortable digestive dishes	P
is beauty cloaked in cadaverous clones?	E
	R
painted obscenely	S
color-clad clowns cavorting clumsily	O
trying to fit the puzzle	N

Maxine Baptiste

WHY?   A
    WHO SAYS the mould cannot be broken?   B
                                                                            L
A   shawl   twirls,   spins,   E
    feet   glance   and   peep   N
        moccasins turn, touch   E
featherlike   S
   swift, sure   S
DRUMS drum as heart and mind chase notions of inexpedience NOT
SONG lifts the spirit toward pride and self-recognition   JUST
                                                                          ON
What matters popular modality, modernity?   THE
Passing, pass, passe.   OUTSIDE

REMEMBER integrity, wholeness, the embodiment of SELF,   Grandmothers
my friend, my sister, my daughter.   Mothers
BEAUTIFUL, BEAUTY DEFINED, OURSELVES   Daughters
                                                                          Sisters
                                                                          Lovers
                                                                          WE ARE

Richard Van Camp

The Hope Of Wolves

    i
You take a child
doused in flames
with steam split skin
a child who knew rape before sleep
and you silence your ears when she cries
YOU!
YOU DID THIS TO ME!
YOU!
and you take it upon yourself to show her the song of trees
when they split the sun
and you give her the peace of sleep
and you point to the place fish bathe
and say this is home to you
this is home
and you tell her to sing to the island where they keep the dogs
that have bitten children
you tell her this
you give her hope
you show her sand
and watch her sniff the air
the way a dog will sniff at fire

    ii
Ask her what her
dreams were before contact
was blue a shade or voice?
and she will tell you of a time when she was a blade dancer
and a wave of her hand
could take a whole room down
she will frown and from the sand
she will pull the hot and bleeding heart of her enemy's chief
as he falls shocked and screaming across the sea

Richard Van Camp

    iii
Your voice is bathing me you will say
and her mouth will be light that will touch your secret place
I am wolf she will say
and you taught me how
she will smile and hold her hands to the face of moon
not to scratch or mar
but to hold and laugh
and dance
and sing...

(this poem is for JB, MSM, GM, FB, TB, WT, and others hurt...)

Edee O'Meara

that sage, she speak to me

that sage
she call me.
she call me to the hills.
smell my blossoms
she say
look at the pretty flowers
growing around me.
sit down and rest
little anishinabe
slow down
and listen to my song.

that sage
she live up on them hill.
she stretches herself
reaching far as she can.
she have relations
all around.
that sage
she make music
swaying with the winds
as she sings a birthing song
under springtime sun.
that sage
she grow tall
higher than me
that one.

that sage
she say
good to see indian around.
they not many comin' by these day.
she say
sit down
smoke your tobacco
look over at that mountain.
she bleeding.

Edee O'Meara

that white man
he cut her
and I don't like to see that
so I send my medicine
with the wind
and that wind
she carry it good
and that mountain
she getting better
so long as that
white man
stay away.

that sage
she seem patient.
she say
not to worry too much.
she say
we headed for hard times
but she gonna help.
she tell me
long time ago
when indian was indian
more time to learn.
these day
indians rushing
full speed
and they get
nowhere
they running so fast
they stepping on each other.

that sage
she speak softly
she tell me
look at my seeds
they my children
they with me for awhile
but soon they leave.

Edee O'Meara

when they with me
they close.
i teach them who they are
and what they are to do.
when they go
i not worried
i content
'cuz i know
i teach them
what they have to know.
they safe
'cuz they understand
where they from
and where they headed.
they know the good medicine.
they know
a lot of indian
to doctor out there.

they there
all around
for the indian.
that sage
she say
they wait
for indians
all the time.
she tell me
they growing strong.
pretty soon
them indian all come back.
she say
they will
find the way again.
that sage
she confident
she say
indian will be indian
again.

Edee O'Meara

she say
one day
them indian
will hold their children close
again.
she say
them indian
will teach them good.
she say
them indian
will show them how
them indian children
will walk a good walk.
they heads will be clear
and they be strong.
them indian children
will not be lost
when they leave their parents
they be indian
like long ago.
them parents won't worry
'cuz they be good parents.
that sage
she tell me
that's how it will be.
she patient.
she say
she just waiting.
but she still teachin' her children.

that sage
she tell me
this day a good one.
she tell me
soon i should come back.
she say
she prepare
to come home with me.
she say

Edee O'Meara

---

today not the day.
gotta nurture her children
she say.
soon they all be ready
to travel
with the indian.
that sage she quiet
she say
that's all for today
she say
thank-you for visiting

that sage
she speak to me

We Three Women

We three women,
we walk in a pack
like wolves
who record
their history
with the eyes
of our ancestors,
with dignity,
with patience.

We three women,
we run together
like a fine chardonnay,
spilling and splashing
against the long-stemmed glass.
We blend as one;
our fine lineage
and blood-line
that reeks of strength,
that beats in our veins
like the pounding
of the oilskin drum
in the distance.

We three women,
the present evidence
of our matrilineal society
and maternal bloodline
we call home,
beckons beyond
our condos, cars and cash-
the clothes we cultivate
contain the rich roads
of our people;
bold with beauty
tradition,
history.

Pamela Dudoward

We wear them well.

We three women
will be standing tall
long after losses suffered
and families falter.
We will weep
with strength and courage,
life and death,
change and choices.
Because we can feel and falter,
we will weep,
we will stand tall
through eternity;
we will lock arms.

We three women,
one by one,
we will pass
to the other side.
Death nor life
shall ever separate
we three women
who walk with weight.

We three women
who connect
to one another
like the great cry
of the eagle,
the seaweed blackness
of the raven,
the mass presence
of the bear,
the swift sureness
of the wolf,
and our crest-
the blatant beauty
of the killer whale.

Pamela Dudoward

We three women,
First Nations force,
we stitch our sadness
and sing our sentiment
through separate slices
we cut our ways-
but always side by side,
thick and thin,
pain and pleasure.
Mother
Sister
Me.
We three women.

Richard Van Camp

My Review of "When the World Was New"

Granny's at Kare-ee-o-kee and Grandpa's asleep. I could watch hockey or I could wake my sister and get her to tell me stories like she used to. She was the one who told me if you cut off a cat's whiskers, it can't see so good afterwards.

I told her if you touch gasoline to a cat's arsehole, it'll jump 12 feet in the air easy. She laugh and chase me around the house, but that was a while ago: now she needs a lot of sleep cuz she study hard for her college entrance exams.

I guess what I'm trying to get at is there's nothing to do these days. Fort Smith is dead. No arcades, they all shut down. Which is sad, cuz I was getting pretty good at "H Factor" and "Shinobi" but I don't miss it too much. I got Nintendo and Sega: Nintendo for my birthday from Auntie Laura and Sega for Christmas from Auntie Sylvie. Auntie Sylvie had her finger slammed in a car when she was about five years old and it stopped growing, so she spruce it up with three rings: she has nice feet though, I can tell you that. Real nice feet, she always wear panty hose and you can see her toes and I like that. Dunno why, but I do. I hope my granny doesn't find out that I like feet. She knows everything else. She found my girlie mag stash, my snuff can, my salvaged smoke butts, and my "Heavy Metal" magazines. I can see why she threw out the first three, but the "Heavy Metal?" Man, that magazine is my life. I'm going to be a comic book artist like McFarlane or Bisley and I know I'm good. Mr. Cameron, my art teacher, hang up every drawing I do in the classroom. I give him so much he have to hang it up in the hallways and I get compliments all the time.

Granny says I should draw eagles and the Dogrib people but they're so boring. None of them have muscles like Richard Corben can draw and none of them have big hooters or blond hair. Just black hair, brown eyes and bannock butts. How bone!

I gotta draw action, not a bunch of Indians sitting at the coffee shop or driving around, 12 in a truck, cruising slow and acting tough. Grandpa, when he could talk, boy, I tell you, he told me some great stories and one day I'm gonna draw what he told me.

I like listening to the elders. They're quiet and don't yell or get excited. I bring them strawberries when they're ripe in July, or rabbits for stew. This one lady I go see, her name is Seraphine Evans. She is Cree. She told me a story about a man who grew up in town, they called him Skinny. He was real ugly and nobody wanted to hang around with him cuz he had a gimpy leg, he kinda wobble around town and every body steer clear of him. Well, I guess something happened to him that made him handsome and he got lots of women. Seraphine say women would follow him around in packs and he was good at cards. He'd win almost every time and that's how he made his living, he didn't have to trap or hunt, he just played cards and laughed with the ladies. Well one day, Seraphine told me, this man, all sharp looking, came to talk to him and say two words. He say, "It's time." and Skinny, he get all sick right away and fall down. That sharp man, he just walk away and Skinny start wailing, "NO! NO! NO!"

Well the nuns had to look after him at the Hostel and Skinny died that night, but before he died, he asked to be blessed by the Bishop and when the Bishop give him his last rites, he say Skinny get this look in his eyes, like he was looking into hell and he throw up lots and lots and he throw up frogs and these frogs hop up the Nuns' legs and they run around the room til the Bishop opened the door and Skinny, he died.

"Poor poor Skinny," Seraphine say over and over. "Poor poor Skinny."

I show Seraphine my pictures and tell her I'm gonna draw Skinny one day seeing Hell and puking frogs and she wink at me and thank me for the rabbits.

It's stories like that keep me going: It keep the Dene going too. Everyone has time for a story and once you tell one, you usually get a storytelling party going and that's just fine with me. It's better than tv and it makes me feel good.

I got a book from the school library. It's called *When the World Was New*. It was written by a Slavey elder named George Blondin. He's from Fort Franklin, that's way up north, real cold and the trees are so skinny, look like they were burnt and are trying to make a comeback. My sister say it's cuz Franklin is so close to the barrenlands, I say fine, sure, whatever (I never been up there so it doesn't mean too much to me.)

Well, George Blondin, he did a great job on this book. It's filled with great stories. He talks about the time there were the Na acho', gigantic mammals, who were dangerous and liked to eat people. He tell a story about Yamoria, the man who put everything right in its place and give us Dene laws to live by. He tell us about a family of eagles that used to eat people and dine on flesh (I like that--dine on flesh.) He had to kill the whole family except one boy eagle and Yamoria told the eagle to eat only fish, and he show him how; and afterwards, he give that boy eagle a squeeze so he won't grow to be a giant like his folks and he stopped growing alright, and that's why there are no more giant eagles. Neat, hey?

The only thing I don't like about this book is the artwork. If they would have hired me, they would have had the best, but as it is, all they got are skinny little stick men inside chucking spears and the caribou! The caribou! They look so sickly and and pitiful! Like a tundra wind would have no trouble at all knocking them over!

> So I get me an idea.
> I want to tell the world about this book
> and I want to do the artwork for some of these stories
> so I do my best
> and they're damn good.

I drew the story George Blondin told about a boy who had strong caribou medicine. It's sad. He loved caribou and asked them to come and get him and they did. And this boy, he was half caribou and half human, he brought that whole caribou herd back to the camp and he sang his mom a sad farewell song to say goodbye to his mother. (Don't tell no one this, but after I read that, I kind of give my mom a hug and tell her I love her.)

Boy that George Blondin, he really gets you good when he wants to make you cry.

So I drew a picture. I called it "Farewell" and I'm mighty proud of it. I drew about Di, a powerful medicine man in our history, who was given a vision--before he was ever born--about his strengths and powers. I call that one "Gift." It's kind of spooky cuz Di is told to cut a tree and he does, and this tree starts to bleed and Di is told to blow smoke from a pipe on the bleeding. After he blows the smoke, the bleeding stops! Just like that! and Di is told that if anyone he knows gets cut or hurt, just to blow smoke and the bleeding would stop. I like that a lot and I drew it fine.

I also drew "War," and I show a fight between the Dene and the Na acho', the giant animals that tried to eat the people.

There's lots more stories in here and I think this is priceless book. There's even a map with all the Dene communities on it with their traditional names and there's explanations on medicine power, Dene law, and teachings for the people.

This one story I like is about "Swallow Medicine." It's about this Dene medicine man who used his powers, but he was kind of weak and every time he do something, he unleash something fierce that swallow children's souls. That medicine man know what's up but he just keep on and lots of children die. The other medicine men got together to find who was doing this to the community and there was a battle. They exposed the "Swallow Medicine" and they killed it dead, roasted it! I wanted to show the battle and a few of the Dene medicine men dying. I call that one "Cleanse."

I want to be able to read this book and tell these stories to my grandchildren and, thanks to George Blondin, I can.

I just think the artwork and cover were done cheap and they look cheap and I bet a lot of people won't give it a chance because of it. But, because of my artwork, and because of this little write-up, I hope you read it and tell all your friends.

I hear George Blondin is working on another book like this one and a children's book too. I hope he sees my artwork and gives me a call cuz here in Fort Smith, I have a lot of paper, a good pen, and acres of time.

Ines Hernandez-Avila

Canto al Parto del Sexto Sol: The Healing and Blessing of Mother Earth and Our Song to Her Birthing of the New Sun of Consciousness and Wisdom

>A nation is not conquered
>until the hearts of the women
>are on the ground
>then it is done
>no matter how strong the weapons
>or how brave the warriors
>   -Cheyenne saying-

MujerTierraNosotras
WeWomanEarthSelves
Rise up from the violence against self against spirit
the violence against the children the old ones all life
We lift up our hearts
We let our hearts lead us to stand up
stand strong in our beauty our power our love
stand strong in the face of terror and fear
stand wise in the face of hatred and confusion
stand powerful in the face of greed and wrath
on behalf of ourselves
on behalf of humanity
on behalf of all that lives all that is

When we Women lift our hearts up from the ground
all nations/peoples are transformed
when WomanSelf says NO to degradation
when WomanSelf says YES to the cleansing
YES to speaking, to making things clear
YES to shaking up the world
unbinding everything that is and was
disconnecting to do
to unleash the fury
to release the pain
to send away forever the humiliating
terrifying behavior that is not becoming human beings
To Be so that our prayers our work our lives our selves

transform the ugliness corruption filth
and so bring change in a good way

We bring healing We bring blessing
with water with incense with herbs yes with flowers
with all that MotherEarth takes to herself
all that comes as gifts from her
As WomanSelf WomanEarth
MujerTierraNosotras rise up
as WE allow our faces to shine forth
as WE give our hearts valor
then the New Sun will emerge
from OurHeart HerHeart
to the rhythm of Our Songs

and our songs will join with the songs of all life
and with HerSong
to receive the Birth
to receive the rays of fire
the luminous sacred arrows of conciencia
that will pierce our serpentbodies
as our quetzalspirits awaken to the wisdom
of yet newer dimensions of life and love

Our ancestors rejoice as we rise
Our families rejoice as we rise and bring them with us
Our relations in the animal, plant, water, stone and sky
worlds rise in relief and in thanksgiving
as we rise to greet this New Light
which we proclaim
with song
with incense
with love
with light
that manifests
with the banners from Our Hearts
that we lift up
as our heads are held high
our faces become radiant
and our spirits soar

Colleen Seymour

AUTUMN LEAVES

Sitting in the room
She smelled the air
as the wind
swept through.
Was this the smell...
the warning
her Grampa had spoken about
when she was eight years old?
She speaks of his prophecy...
today!
She speaks in a learned
eighty-eight year old voice.

She heard "her" elected people.
They spoke of unity
meanwhile
the meeting happened
in a plush hotel conference room.

Where were 'our' people?

As an act of respect
the elected chief said,
"Now I am honored
to introduce you to one of our elders."

Granny...

Granny observed her son.
"My people" she said,
as she directed her loving look
to her son's eyes.
"Today, I am worried
we are speaking of our
people's water rights
here in this rich room."

"Yes,
I am your elder.
Therefore, I have a mind
to get the nearest red willow
and whip you all the way home.
We have our own meeting hall,
at home.
'Our' people will be more
than happy to listen there.
Now git, my son!"

The interpreter,
another of her children
blushed.

Hours later
on the people's land
the meeting continued
on water rights.

Granny is getting on.
She has seen the other side
of the veil.
Her ancestors
say,
Remember...
Just remember, what we spoke of.

Preface

I never liked my mother's mother, Leona May Baker. When we would visit her and my grandfather in their two-room house in northwestern Arkansas where they were sharecroppers, she would awaken me long before I was ready to get up. I would be irritable with lack of sleep as she would sit by my bed and catalogue the gruesome details of every death of every relative and friend as well as each event of personal disaster within her known landscape.

My grandmother was half-Cherokee and Irish and was orphaned at a very young age and raised by fullblood Cherokees in Jay, Oklahoma. She gave birth to six sons and one daughter-my mother. Each birth added to the burden of life. Once she took out a gun and shot at all of them as they ran through the trees to get away from her. My mother recalls the sounds of bullets flying by her head. She disliked my mother.

My grandfather, Desmond Baker, left to work on the railroad when they were especially destitute. While he was away my grandmother had an affair. When he returned nine months later she was near full-term with a baby who wasn't his. He beat her until she went into labor and gave birth to the murdered child.

Shortly after the killing, my grandparents attempted double suicide. They stood on the tracks while a train bore down on them as all the children watched in horror. At the last possible second my grandfather pushed my grandmother off to safety and leaped behind her.

With the impending birth of my son's daughter, I was prompted to find out more about this grandmother who I had never made peace with-My mother told me of her incredible gift of storytelling, how she would keep the children entranced for weeks by tales she would invent-they had no books, television or radio. And then she told me the baby murder story and train story.

I began to have compassion for this creative woman who was weighted down with seven children and no opportunities. Maybe her affair was the lightness she needed to stay alive.

When my granddaughter Haleigh was born, I felt the spirit of this grandmother in the hospital room. Her presence was a blessing.

I welcomed her.

THE NAMING
for Haleigh Sara Bush

I think of names that have profoundly changed the direction of disaster. Of the raw whirling wind outlining femaleness emerging from the underworld.

It blesses the frog taking refuge under the squash flower cloud, the stubborn weeds leaning in the direction of wind bringing rain.

My grandmother is the color of night as she tells me to move away from the window when it is storming. The lightning will take you.

I thought it was my long dark hair appearing as lightning. The lightning appears to be relatives.

Truth can appear as disaster in a land of things unspoken. It can be reached with white arrows, each outlining the meaning of delicate struggle.

And can happen on a night like this when the arrow light is bitten by sweet wind.

My grandmother took leave years ago by way of her aggravated heart. I haven't seen her since, but her warnings against drownings, lightning or anything else portending death by sudden means still cling to my ears.

I take those risks against the current of warning as if she had invented negative space of wind around the curve of earth.

That night after my granddaughter-born-for-my-son climbed from the underworld we could smell ozone over the lake made of a few centuries of rain.

I went hunting for the right name and found the spirit of the ice age making plans in the bottom of the lake. Eventually the spirit will become rain, remake the shoreline with pines and laughter.

Joy Harjo

In the rain I saw the child who was carried by lightning to the other side of the storm. I saw my grandmother who never had any peace in this life blessed with animals and songs.

Oh daughter-born-of-my-son, of my grandmother, of my mother; I name you all these things:

The bag of white arrows is heavy with rain.

The earth is wet with happiness.

Mekwehc Niciy

I say Mekwehc for all the things
you have taught me
Mekwehc for all the things
you have made me see
Mekwehc for all the things
you made me feel
Mekwehc for helping me to
seek and understand the dreams
I once disregarded
Mekwehc for helping me the
times I was in pain
Mekwehc for helping me the
times I was lonely
Mekwehc for all the laughs
we have shared
Mekwehc for helping me to
recognize who I am
Mekwehc for helping me learn how
to care
Mekwehc for helping me learn how
to share
Mekwehc for helping me learn how
to cry
Mekwehc for showing me how
to talk to the Creator
Mekwehc for showing me respect
Kihci Mekwehc Niciy
for pulling that false mask
off my face
which I've worn for so long

Willow Barton

For the Child-heart

On darker nights, I hold the candle to the sweetgrass
to send prayers on smokey wings toward the sky and God.
I pray that I stay the child, a cup awaiting color.
Hold tender the yellow song of the summer wind
for all its fluted notes rise and fall upon the land
and too, the loons' blue song shimmers on the water.

Such sweet trust the child knows.
The divining willow will find water.
And yes, fairy queens and magic ravens do dance upon the grass.
Certainly it's true
Sleeping shamans lie beneath the land
and in their stirrings send drum-rolls into the sky.
What child would deny
that winter rides the horse of the cold north wind
or that Thunders' drum has many sounds and lightning colours?

Such sweet trust. The settlers had good reason
to search for the colour of freedom. Yes.
In coming here they tested the water.
A new beginning was born a bird rising on the wind.

Such sweet trust. The Indians did not feel they owned the land.
The lupine meadows and the silver birch were colours
of freedom, belonging to all like the water, the sky
and no star configuration could point to the allotment. Certainly,
the many tribes as numerous as the grass,
would never believe anyone but God could split the water, snare the wind.

Such sweet trust every child knows.
The kite will catch the wind.
Somehow there is magic here and upon the land
where the promise of spring begins with the turning of grass.
For the child's innocence knows skin is only colour.
Beneath life's cycles we are only clay and water
and our souls like kites inevitably reach for the sky.

Willow Barton

On darker nights,
I hold the candle to the sky and the wind to send up prayers,
sweetgrass offerings from the land, to God.
I pray with a child's eyes we see the sweetgrass is for all. God
give us a child's vision to see the colours of the land,
moving with our hearts song, shimmering on the water.
God keep the child who sends prayers toward the sky.

God see our prayers that drift to the sky.
Kites held high, though bound to the land
they send our prayers into the wind.
Streamers of earth-bound colour they hold our hearts
so we may bless the water, the grass.

Beth Cuthand

Post-Oka Kinda Woman

Here she comes strutting down your street.
This Post-Oka woman don't take no shit.

She's done with victimization, reparation,
degradation, assimilation,
devolution, coddled collusion,
the "plight of the Native Peoples."

Post-Oka woman, she's o.k.
She shashay into your suburbia.
MacKenzie Way, Riel Crescent belong to her
like software, microwave ovens,
plastic Christmas trees and lawn chairs.

Her daughter wears Reeboks and works out.
Her sons cook and wash up.
Her grandkids don't sass their Kohkom!
No way.

She drives a Toyota, reads bestsellers,
sweats on weekends, colors her hair,
sings old songs, gathers herbs.
Two steps Tuesdays,
Round dances Wednesdays,
Twelve steps when she needs it.

Post-Oka woman she's struttin' her stuff
not walkin' one step behind her man.
She don't take that shit
Don't need it!   Don't want it.
You want her   then treat her right.

Talk to her of post-modern deconstructivism
She'll say: "What took you so long?"

You wanna discuss Land Claims?

Beth Cuthand

She'll tell ya she'd rather leave
her kids with a struggle than a bad settlement.

Indian Government?
        Show her cold hard cash.

Tell her you've never talked to a real live "Indian"
    She'll say: "Isn't that special."

Post-Oka woman, she's cheeky.
    She's bold.   She's cold.

And she don't take no shit!
No shit.

Lori New Breast

FULL-TIME JOB

A brother of mine,
    walks quickly down a street.
the relatives of dead and living Indian fighters
    wait upon his arrival.
hungry and trembling their stomachs sound with desire,
    for Grandma's drum, dress, and bones.
      I slip in and out of the shadows
      of the night.
she is singing from inside the grocery sack,
    tucked underneath his arm.
Indian man and an unknown heiress.
      I have tracked them since the liberation rally,
      following the trail of his footprints
          and her credit card receipts.

I cradle the spirit arrow
    Grandma left in my dream.
he looks past my body, hair and eyes,
    as I match the beat of his stride.
        a tap on the shoulder,
          I slice his flesh right above his heart.
      with a rustling of paper,
    I clutch her to my body.

I count coup,
    as surprise grips his face and mind,
Grandma's sweet laughter rings in his ears.
      he flees down a street,
        thinking the night hides his retreat.

Colin T. Jarrett

REACH OUT - A Song

How do we heal those wounds
    so deep,
When they affect us so bad
    we cannot sleep.
Reach out, reach out!

How do we shatter the walls
    of silence,
with gentleness and caring,
    without the violence.
    Reach out, reach out!

How can we speak
    instead of just talk,
when we reach these barriers
    we must not balk.
    Reach out, reach out!

How can we break
    the chains of fear,
when we think all the world
    will just jeer and sneer!
    Reach out, reach out!

How can we embrace
    the courage to change
with gentle compassion
    within our range.
Reach out, reach out!

How can we handle
    the discomfort of growing
to unclog the channels
    and get our Love flowing.
Reach out, reach out!

Colin T. Jarrett

How do we smash
    all yesterdays troubles
to become new people
and rebuild the rubble!
Reach out, reach out!

How can we reach
    the place of calm healing
maybe with love and acceptance
we can discover the feeling.
    Reach out, reach out.

If we all go together
    with one common way
we can help each other
    day by day.

Suddenly we find the road
    to Life True
is caring and sharing
    with you, you, and you.

For reaching out brings
    wholeness so strong
to enable us to have
peaceful lives so long.

William George

ORIGIN STREAM (West Coast Rhythm)

Using all my resources to reclaim breath
moments slice through stream
wraps me in its embrace
moments past
moments present

Stream is here
stream is always here
sends its challenge
its invitation to tap its flow
I immerse myself in the cascading currents
moments channel through me

In front of me and behind me
dead memories
always out of reach
unretainable in its purest form

The stream in front of me is dry

Outside of my periphery
a bountiful stream emerges
washes over me
washes through me

This stream is of me
this stream is me
generations flow
I am enmeshed in the waves of memories renewed

I stand on stream's bank
winds blow
dance me
moments dance
wind catches me embrace
breath in and exhale renewed
hhoo   hhoo   hhoo

William George

I am the blood that flows through the veins of my grandmothers
I am the blood that flows through the veins of my grandfathers
I am the blood that flows down the mountains
I am the blood that flows out to sea

    I am the rain that flows across the land
    cleansing rain healing rain
    connects me with the winged ones
        with the four legged
        with the gilled ones
        with the two legged
        with cedar
        with the wind
        with sky
connects me with Mother Earth

Earth	Mother	
Sky	Mother	
Sun	Mother	
Wind	Mother	
Rain	Mother	
Wolf	Mother	
Cedar	Mother	
Salmon	Mother	
Longhouse	Mother	
Clan	Mother	
Nation	Mother	
Universe	Mother	
Song/Dance	Mother	
Dream/Rhythm	Mother	
Creation	Mother	
Origin	Mother	breathes

hhoo   hhoo   hhoo

Yellow cedar breath
red cedar breath carved
cedar   movement
cedar   survival
cedar   bowls

William George

cedar   masks
cedar   boxes
cedar   poles
cedar   bark   offerings
cedar   dreams
cedar   voices
hhoo   hhoo   hhoo
cedar paddle slices through ocean salt spray
cedar canoe journeys ocean
hhoo   hhoo   hhoo
paddler pumps cedar canoe along water's course

wet, misty vapours wash over self
wash over the land
rain's cleansing release
rain's healing embrace
rain   dreams
rain   drops
rain   growth
rain   past present future
rain   changes
rain   emerges
rain   strength
seeyaam
there is strength in tears
there is strength in grieving

I am the tear drops that stream down the cheeks of my ancestors

    I am the cedar that reaches to embrace tomorrow
    roots stretch from creation
    branches stretch into generations to come

    I am the salmon that cycle from river to ocean
    and ocean to river
    swims
    endures
    passes cycle to cycle
    always journeys

William George

reclaiming breath connection through the ages

I am origin that flows from the beginnings to present
I am origin that asserts its teachings in Story
I am the Creation of the universe
it is my passing that is celebrated in Story
it is my passing that is passed down in Storytelling

I am the wind that sings elders home
I am the wind that sings to newborn

I am the soil humankind tread on
I am the soil the four legged set upon
I am the soil where cedar plants its being

I am the stone that is of the earth
I am the stone that is blood of the earth

I am the sun that warms the land
I am the sun that lights the day

  Origin is the stream
flows from the beginnings
     shimmers cascades through the ages
       shimmers cascades through the generations
        wraps me in its embrace
         invites me to tap its flow
           Origin is the stream that flows beneath me
          beneath the earth
              Origin stream flows through my veins

Biographies of Gatherings V Authors

Janice Acoose is from the Sakimay (Saulteaux) First Nation and the Marival Metis community. Currently, she is an Assistant Professor of English with the Saskatchewan Indian Federated College. She has been previously published in journals and anthologies.

Jeannette Armstrong is Okanagan, residing on the Penticton Indian Reservation. She has a degree in Fine Arts from the University of Victoria. She has been anthologized numerously and has published poetry and articles in a wide variety of journals.

Sheilia Austin was born and raised and is living on the Tsartlip Reserve on Vancouver Island, B.C. She is mother of two daughters, ages 8 years and 11 years. Sheila had a 20 year teaching career for Grades K-7.

Marie Annharte Baker is a poet, storyteller, gynocratic granny. She is a student at U of Winnipeg in playwriting and women's literature. Her healed but humble hope is to decolonize Native writing through personal essays, and occasional storytelling theater performance.

Maxine Baptiste is an Okanagan from Oliver, B.C. She has had previous works published in the *Gatherings* Journals. She is currently working towards a degree in linguistics. She is a firm believer in the preservation of aboriginal languages.

Willow Barton (Gail Duiker) was born in Red Pheasant, Saskatchewan (Yellow Sky). She is of Cree, Norwegian and Sioux ancestory. Writing words and drawing has become her way of communicating emotion and circumstance.

Arlene Marie Beaumont is an Ojibway who grew up in a small town in northwestern Ontario. She is currently working with autistic adults. Her work is also an attempt to testify and honour the struggles of Native people.

Biographies

Don Birchfield is a member of the Choctaw Nation of Oklahoma, is a graduate of the University of Oklahoma College of Law. His 10,000 word essay, *Choctaw Nation*, is forthcoming in the *1995 GALE Encyclopedia of Multicultural America*.

Kimberly M. Blaeser (Anishinabe) is an enrolled member of the Minnesota Chippewa Tribe and grew up on White Earth Reservation. She has published personal essays, poetry, short fiction, journalism and scholarly articles in various journals and collections.

Peter Blue Cloud/Aroniawenrate is a member of the Mohawk Nation at Kahnawake, Mohawk Territory. He has 7 books published including *Elderberry Flute Song* (White Pine Press, 1989) and *The Other Side of Nowhere* (White Pine Press, 1991).

A. Rodney Bobiwash, an Anishinabe (Ojibway) from the Thessalon Reserve on the north shore of Lake Huron, in Northern Ontario.

Dorothy Christian is from the Okanagan - Shuswap Nations. She was born and raised on the Spallumcheen reservation in B.C. Dorothy is working on completing a double major in Political Science and Religious Studies in the Honours Program at the University of Toronto. She is currently living in Penticton, B.C.

Marcia Crosby is Haida from Massett, B.C. She has a BA in studio arts and literature and is completing a M.A. in social art history at the University of British Columbia. Ms. Crosby is publishing an article in *Vancouver Anthology: The Institutional Politics of Art*, and co-editing a special women's issue of the *Capilano Review*.

Beth Cuthand was born in Northern Saskatchewan. She is a poet, educator and activist of the Little Pine Cree Nation. Her most recent collection of poetry, *Voices in the Waterfall* is published by Theytus Books Ltd. Beth completed her M.F.A. in Creative Writing at the University of Arizona. She teaches at the En'owkin International School of Writing in Penticton, B.C.

Biographies

Kateri Damm is a band member of the Chippewas of Nawash, Cape Croker Band on Georgian Bay, Ontario and of mixed Ojibway/Polish Canadian/Pottawotami/English descent. She was born in Toronto. Kateri received her Honour's B.A. in English Literature at York University in 1987. *My Heart Is A Stray Bullet* was her first collection of poetry.

Christopher David is a member of the Tsartlip Band on Vancouver Island. He is a graduate of the En'owkin International School of Writing in Penticton, B.C. Christopher divides his time between writing and managing a cappucino stand on his rez.

Pamela Dudoward is a Tsimshian writer who lives in Vancouver. Her work has appeared *Gatherings Vol IV*. She is currently employed by the Ministry of Social Services and is a member of the board at the Vancouver Aboriginal Friendship Centre Society. She is the co-founder of the Aboriginal Personnel Employment Network.

Valerie Dudoward is a Tsimshian writer who lives and works in Vancouver. She is a playwright and poet whose work has been professionally staged and published in various anthologies and high school textbooks, including *Gatherings Vol. IV*. She is currently working on her first short novel.

Jack Forbes is the Director of Native Studies at the University of California, his tribal affiliations are Delaware - Lenpa and Powhantan - Renape. His latest book is entitled *Columbus and Cannibals*.

Jose Garza is of Coahuilteca/Mexican and Lipan Apache heritage. He lives in western Pennsylvania.

William George is from the Tsleil-Waututh, Burrard Inlet Band in North Vancouver, B.C. He is a recent graduate of the En'owkin International School of Writing Program. William is currently working on his first manuscript and a literary project with his community.

Donna Kahenrakwas Goodleaf, ED.D. is a citizen of the Kanienkehaka (Mohawk) Nation, Kahnawake Territory. She currently teaches at the En'owkin International School of Writing in Penticton, B.C. Her book *Entering The Warzone: A Mohawk Perspective on Resisting Invasion* will be published by Theytus Books Ltd. in the Fall, 1994.

Raven Hail is an active member of the Cherokee Nation. Her poetry and essays on Cherokee culture have appeared in various publications. She has also written 3 novels and a cook book.

Louise Halfe, whose Cree name is Sky Dancer, was born on the Saddle Lake Reserve in Alberta. Louise has a Bachelor of Social Work from the University of Regina. She is an award winning poet and the author of *Bear Bones and Feathers* (Coteau Books, 1994).

Leona Hammerton is of the Shuswap Nation and resides on the Adams Lake reserve. She is a graduate of the En'owkin International School of Writing. Leona will begin her fourth year of the Native Indian Teachers Education Program at U.B.C.

Joy Harjo was born in Tulsa, Oklahoma in 1951 and is an enrolled member of the Creek Tribe. She received her M.F.A. in Creative Writing from the Iowa Writer's Workshop at the University of Iowa in 1978. She is the author of 5 books of poetry. Joy will release a CD this spring with her band, Poetic Justice.

A.A. Hedge Coke is mixed-blood (Huron; Tsalagi; French Canadian; Portuguese...). She is currently a corresponding student in the MFA in Writing program at Vermont College. Her full-length poetry manuscript is being retained by a leading press, her full-length play is a a finalist in a major competition, and her novel-in-progress is a semi-finalist in line for a working fellowship.

Ines Hernandez-Avila is an enrolled member of the Colville Confederated Tribal Reservation. She is Nimipu (Nez Perce) of Joseph's band on her mom's side and Tejana (Chicana) on her dad's side. She is an Assistant Professor of Native American Studies at the University of California at Davis.

Biographies

Jane Inyallie is Carrier Sekani. She was the co-editor of a Theytus anthology *Shadows*. Jane has graduated from the En'owkin International School of Writing in Penticton, B.C. She plans to complete her first manuscript of poetry by the Winter of 1995.

Carrie Jack is Okanagan from Penticton, B.C. She has previously been published in *Gatherings* Vol. III and Vol. IV.

Colin Thomas Jarrett, poet, is an Aborigine of the Gumnaingyyirn Tribe of people. Colin is also part American or Canadian Indian (unsure which, at this time). Colin lives and writes from the Bellwood Aboriginal Reserve in Australia.

Debby Keeper is a Cree from the Fisher River First Nation in the Interlake area of Manitoba. Debby is a visual artist currently completing the third year of her Bachelor of Fine Arts Degree (Honors) Program at the University of Manitoba.

Sarah Jane King, is an Ojibway woman who currently resides in Red Lake, Ontario, Canada.

Anna Kruger is Okanagan and a member of the Penticton Indian Band. She was born in 1961 and is the mother of 4 children. Anna is employed with the En'owkin Centre in Penticton, B.C. She hopes to further her career in the educational field.

Mary Lawrence is an Okanagan, born in Tonasket, Washington and raised on the Okanagan Reserve in Vernon, B.C. She is a recent graduate of the En'owkin International School of Writing in Penticton, B.C. and she is working towards a Bachelor of Fine Arts at the University of Victoria.

Jim Logan is a painter/poet who divides his residence between Kamloops, B.C. and Millbrook, Nova Scotia. He is Metis, born 1955 in New Westminster, B.C.

Sarah Lyons is a mixedblood of Isleta, Pueblo descent. She lives in Portland, Oregon where she works as an office assistant at a local University.

Biographies

Victoria Lena Manyarrows is Eastern Cherokee and 38 years old, and was raised alongside reservations and within mixed communities in North Dakota and Nebraska. As a writer, activist and artist, her goal is to use written and visual images to convey and promote a positive Native-based world view.

duncan mccue was born in 1971, of Anishinabe heritage, from Ontario. He is currently studying law at UBC, and working for the television program 'YTV News.'

Duncan Mercredi (Inninu) is Cree from the Misipawistik (Grand Rapids) First Nation. He currently lives in Winnipeg, Manitoba. Duncan has been published in various anthologies.

Morningstar Mercredi is Dene from Fort Chipewyan, Alberta. Morningstar is a storyteller, actress, freelance model, playwright and poet. She attended the En'owkin International School of Writing.

Henry Michel is Secwepemc from the Sugar Cane Reserve in central B.C. He teaches Adult Basic Education in Penticton, B.C. Henry has 3 poems published in *Seventh Generation*, Theytus Books and has 1 poem in *Voices under one Sky*, Nelson Canada Ltd.

Cammy-Jo Mulvahill is a member of the Tsilhqot'in Nation. Having grown up in non-Native society, she felt lost among her own people. Upon entering the Native Indian Teacher Education Program, she has been able to explore her Native self.

Lori New Breast is an enrolled member of the Blackfeet Nation. She is completing her M.A. in Ethnic Studies at San Francisco State University. She loves dancing to the drum, and creating traditional regalia.

Paul Ogresko is 36 years old from the Willow Cree First Nation in central Saskatchewan. He has worked as a journalist, writer and editor in Toronto.

Biographies

Jacqueline Oker is a Beaver Indian from the Doig River Reserve near Fort St. John, B.C. Presently a student in the En'owkin International School of Writing in Penticton, B.C. She is 28 years old.

Gunargie O'Sullivan is from the Kwakuilth Nation, in Alert Bay. She is the proud mother of a daughter, Nimkish O'Sullivan-YoungIng. Gunargie is an actress studying at the En'owkin International School of Writing exploring her talents as a visual artist and writer.

Edee O'Meara is Anishinabe from Manitoba. She is a second year student at the En'owkin International School of Writing.

Cheryl Ann Payne, a 24 year-old, Inupiaq Eskimo/mixed blood woman of the Americas. Her Inuplaq name is Kylee Bautnuq Punguk. She is attending the University of California at Davis in Native American Studies.

Judy Peck, (Pretty Rock Woman) is Nlaka'pamux and Silx, she was born in the Nicola Valley. In 1990, she received her Bachelor of Education at the University of British Columbia.

Jeannine Peru is Metis born in Saint Boniface, Manitoba. She is currently working on a compilation of her short stories.

Roma Potiki: Te Aupouri, Te Rarawa, Ngati Rangitihi. Roma Potiki is a writer, director and visual artist. She is artistic director of He Ara Hou Theatre Maori Inc. and also works as a consultant. She is resident in Paekakariki and has two children aged 6 and 10.

Sharron Proulx is a Metis of Mohawk, French, Irish ancestry. Sharron has completed her M.A. in Creative Writing and is currently working on her second book. She lives in Calgary.

Gloria Roberds is an Okanagan from Vernon, B.C. She has completed the Creative Writing Certificate at the En'owkin International School of Writing. This fall, Gloria will attend University of Victoria Arts Department. Her career goal is to be an Archival-Researcher for the first Okanagan Indian Museum.

Biographies

Odilia Galvan Rodriguez (Lipan Apache\Chicana) became a writer and political activist early in life. She currently lives with her 8 year old son Hawk in San Francisco Bay Area. Her writings have appeared in several anthologies, magazines and literary journals.

Armand Garnet Ruffo is Ojibway from Chapleau, Northern Ontario. He currently divides his time between Northern Ontario, Ottawa, and Penticton, B.C. where he is an instructor at the En'owkin International School of Writing. Armand's first book of poetry <u>Opening In The Sky</u> is published by Theytus Books Ltd.

Colleen Seymour is a Secwepemc from Kamloops. She is very honoured to be working at a school which strongly supports Secwepemc Immersion in all aspects.

Trixie Te Arama Menzies, born 1936 in Wellington, is a New Zealander of Tainui and Scottish descent. She is taking a break from full-time teaching this year.

Russell Teed is a Metis from Yellowknife, N.W.T. He is presently a student in the En'owkin International School of Writing in Penticton, B.C. Russell is 32 years old.

Kelly Terbasket is a member of the Similkameen band of the Okanagan Nation. She is a part-time student at the En'owkin Centre and is a full-time mother of Madeline, a 11 month old baby. These poems are Kelly's first published works.

Jan Waboose is an Anishinabe Ojibway Writer. She has had writings published in <u>Sweet Grass Road</u> (Native Women's Resource) and <u>The Colour Of Resistance</u> (Sister Vision Press). She is from Northern Ontario.

Jean Wasegijig is Odawa Ojibway, from the Wikwemikong Reserve in central Ontario. Jean graduated from Douglas College in New Westminster, B.C. with a diploma in Association of Applied Arts. She is a researcher and writer.

Biographies

Bernelda Wheeler is of Cree, Assiniboine, Saulteaux, French and Scots ancestry. Her works in progress include a play for children, 8 children's books and a collection of her writing through a long career in communication arts.

Gerry William is a member of the Spallumcheen Indian Band. He currently teaches English and Creative Writing classes at the En'owkin International School of Writing in Penticton, B.C. *The Black Ship*, the first in a series of novels under the general title of *Enid Blue Starbreaks* is being published by Theytus Books Ltd. Gerry is currently completing the third novel in this series.

Richard Van Camp is Dogrib Dene from the Northwest Territories. His first book, *The Lesser Blessed* is currently being edited for publication by Theytus Books.

Other Contributors

George Anderson
Sheila Dick
Darril Guy Le Camp
Pauline Mattess

Artist Statements

Debby Keeper

I choose to deal with my feelings of anger, loss, frustration and sadness in a positive way; through artistic expression, whether it be writing, painting, performance, or video. I hope that young people facing difficult times will find a constructive way to channel their feelings rather than turning to alcohol, solvents, drugs, and suicide. No matter how people treat you, your art will always be there for you to accept whatever you choose to express.

Edee O'Meara

My artwork comes from my spirit. My art helps me to see things from a different aspect. Painting is a new part of my life that I have only discovered in the past year. This is a part of me that keeps my spirit strong and alive.

June Paul

I was born in the Okanagan and I have lived here all my life. My greatest opportunity was to study in the En'owkin International School of Writing, Fine Arts Program. The native influence helped my own style to emerge. My biggest influence came from seeing R.C. Gorman's images of women. I became aware that I wanted to draw images of women. I wanted to bring out their strengths and beauty. As a native woman, I have the need to express womanhood through the symbol of Mother Earth, the importance of women to our culture and to each other.

ACKNOWLEDGEMENTS

Trixie Te Arama Menzies "Karanga" reprinted from *Papakainga* by Trixie Te Arama Menzies with permission of the author.

Trixie Te Arama Menzies "Nga Roimata" reprinted from *Rerenga* by Trixie Te Arama Menzies with permission of the author.

Roma Potiki "Snake Woman Came to Visit" and "to tangi" reprinted from *Stones in Her Mouth* by Ronia Potiki with permission of the author.

Marcia Crosby "Speak Sm'algyax Grandma, Speak Haida Grandpa" reprinted from *Sharing Our Experience* edited by the Canadian Advisory Council on the Status of Women with permission of the author.

Artist's Description

COVER:

Edee O'Meara
Turtle, 1994
Acrylic on paper
14" x 23"

My thoughts were of a beautiful strong woman. This turtle came to me showing me the power of friendship, healing, love. This turtle is old, wise, power.

WATER

Debby Keeper
Lunar Rites, 1993
Relief (Woodcut) on rice paper
67.2 cm x 36.2 cm

Lunar Rites is symbolic of the moon and its importance in the regulation of the woman's cycle. The three figures represent the past, present and future; a continuance of the cycle of life and learning passed down from one generation to the next.

EARTH:

June Paul
Mother Earth, Earth Mother, 1994
India ink and wash on paper

In this piece I faced the woman symbolizing Mother Earth looking into the picture to allow women to view her as themselves. As keeper of the land Mother Earth's blanket and fringes flow and connect with the trees and hills. The symbols on her blanket represent

Okanagan pictographs. The sun becomes a part of the landscape. The eagle represents guidance and wisdom within our legends. The moon represents womanhood and the teachings. The reflection of grandmother represents our greatest teacher to women. She helps us understand what we need to know about our strengths, the power of acceptance, our pride, our values, and about love. In this particular piece my grandmother has been a great influence. She is with me forever.

CHILDREN

Joshua O'Meara, Age: 4
Untitled
Unknown

It means to me that this is my spirit. The tree symbolizes good stuff.

WIND

Debby Keeper
Not Dead, 1992
India ink, taperraser on paper
28 cm x 20.5 cm

Not Dead... explores the issue of child sexual abuse and the human spirit's ability to survive. The sexless centre figure is representative of both genders. The absence of sexual organs on the figure signifies a need for safety; the hope that their abuser will no longer find them desirable and therefore may cease sexually molesting them. The surrounding text expresses some of the feelings a survivor may experience.

FIRE

Debby Keeper
In Two Worlds, 1993
Relief (lineoleum cut) black & white
57 cm x 63 cm

"In Two Worlds" is a play on words and deals with the physical and spiritual transformation of Aboriginal people and their children, the Metis. In the physical world of existence, many people of Aboriginal descent find themselves caught between two worlds; one of ancient and traditional customs and a modern world that still shuns and rejects them. On a spiritual level, some of our people are torn between the religious practices of the Western world (Christianity, and Catholicism) and the religious practices and ceremonies of our own Nations of Aboriginal Peoples. However, there are some who equally and successfully manage to integrate both.